Edward Waterman Evans

Walter Savage Landor

a critical study - Vol. 1

Edward Waterman Evans

Walter Savage Landor
a critical study - Vol. 1

ISBN/EAN: 9783337314934

Printed in Europe, USA, Canada, Australia, Japan

Cover: Foto ©Andreas Hilbeck / pixelio.de

More available books at **www.hansebooks.com**

WALTER SAVAGE LANDOR

A CRITICAL STUDY

BY

EDWARD WATERMAN EVANS, JR.

UNIVERSITY FELLOW, PRINCETON

G. P. PUTNAM'S SONS

NEW YORK
27 West Twenty-third St.

LONDON
24 Bedford St., Strand

The Knickerbocker Press

1892

Printed and Bound by
The Knickerbocker Press, New York
G. P. PUTNAM'S SONS

CONTENTS.

v

PREFACE.

ONLY those books endure as living presences, and not as mere mortuary tablets, wherein there is a vital coalescence of sense and thought, of nature and spirit. Other volumes may possess a relative longevity, as links in a historical development, or as affording suggestive material which shall subsequently be transmuted into artistic form ; but their mortality is inevitable. Scientific knowledge, with its classification of phenomena and its discovery of their necessary co-existences and sequences in time and space, is ever expanding. Hence the latest book in science is usually the best. It has assimilated, and re-

produced in fuller growth, all previous works pertaining to its depart-
ment. Ideas, on the other hand,
that are formed in the crucible of
art—ideas that suffuse the appear-
ances of nature with the free soul of
man—have an absolute value. And
the book embodying them is a spiritual organism, whose end is focused
in itself, in its own delightful, imaginative marriage of idea and expression. The work of art grows not. It
is a " wavering apparition " fixed " in
its place with thoughts that stand
forever."

Now the productions of Walter
Savage Landor are eminently artistic. Hence, as those who admire
him keep noting with approval the
recent reprints of his several works,
and the eulogistic references at present so often made to this master of
English ; they cannot withhold their
belief in his much-doubted predic-

tion, that he, as an author, would dine late surrounded by a choice company of kindred spirits—they cannot withhold their belief that he belongs among the immortals. Though his lettered contemporaries from Southey to Swinburne were almost unanimous in acknowledging the distinction and charm of Landor's writings, his audience, at least until recently, has been by no means proportionate to his commanding worth as a literary artist.

While there have appeared two biographies of Landor, a cumbersome one by John Forster, his literary executor, and a judicious one by Mr. Colvin in the English Men of Letters series, no critique, at once adequately exclusive and inclusive, has been written in the effort to determine Landor's place and function in literature. Unlike a biography, such a critique would have to be exclusive, passing over all details of outward history not inseparably linked with the author's inner life and writings; and it would have to be inclusive, tracing with more coherence than could well be done in a biography the relation of the author's works to his age and to his personality, and then bringing the canons of criticism to bear concretely upon his several contributions in poetry or prose. This has been the method pursued, however tentatively, in the following critical study.

In treating of Landor's attitude toward the scientific, philosophical, and religious conceptions of the period, as also toward criticism and politics, it was found hard to characterize him other than negatively. His positive qualities, however, having thus been provided with a negative background, can, it is hoped, be thereupon brought out in clearer relief.

Though the immediate purpose in writing this critique, and also the Landorian idyl contained in the Appendix, was to compete for college prizes,—one in criticism, the other in poetry,—the aspirations of the writer continued to go out toward a wider audience. And though the actual composition was undertaken and completed amidst the press and distraction of undergraduate duties, these essays are the record of a previous study of Landor's works, at once careful, prolonged, and enthusiastic.

PRINCETON COLLEGE,
    January 13, 1892.

I.

LANDOR AS A MAN OF LETTERS

I.

LANDOR AS A MAN OF LETTERS.

A UNIVERSAL library has three alcoves. The first contains the religious books, those which relate man to Deity. The deepest question in the human soul is the why of its existence ; and the only answer to this riddle of the sphinx is God. Moreover, while the clear-minded Greek may conceive of Divinity as pure intelligence unperturbed by emotion, a passionless force in itself unmoral, because in it duty and inclination are one ; while the vehement Hebrew may picture Jehovah as frowning in righteous anger at the sins of his people,—both Oriental and Occi-

3

dental alike must ever be feeling after the guardian hand of God : and those seers, who have caught a glimpse of his trailing garments, are always to be regarded as the rarest benefactors of mankind. Nor dare we suppose that the Deity has revealed himself once for all far back in the immutable past, that long since the book of God's plan has been sealed. In these modern times, Fichte and Schelling, Carlyle and Emerson, Wordsworth and Browning, these and many more have sought to uncover the secret things of God. The second alcove is stored with those books which unite the mind of man with outward nature. Our ideal of the good is only satisfied by resting in the perfection of the Godhead ; in the same way a type of the true and fair is, upon occasion, best unveiled beneath the shows of nature ; and the Infinite Reason that gleams from moonlit waters, or looks down upon us from the silent stars, has power to rouse our deepest, most impersonal emotions, to soothe our world-weariness, and to attune our souls to the Soul whose manifestation is nature. The third alcove is laden with the humanistic books, the volumes which give the biography of man, his outer and his inner experience.

It would be hard to find more universal categories by which to determine the genus of an author than these. And as criticism too often confines itself to details and technique, thus failing to give an adequate conception even of these, because of its circumscribed point of view, it is well to recognize at the beginning the limitations of our author, and frankly to acknowledge that Walter Savage Landor saw but rarely the under and spiritual side of

nature, and that at no time could
he be called a man of God, having
no final word of the Lord to utter.
And while these three classes of
books are not always mutually exclusive, but resemble water circles,
each of which ripples into the other,
yet, like such circles, each class retains a measure of its own identity.
Thus, though Wordsworth was mentioned as an interpreter of "the
ways of God to men," he stands pre-
eminently as the poet of nature.
Precisely so is Landor, above all,
the humanist. Masculine strength
and maidenly tenderness, all the
variations of noble and attractive
character, excited in him deep interest; and his interest was gauged
by his insight. Landor's very defi-
ciency as an abstract thinker, his
inability to forge a chain of dialectic,
left his imagination the more un-
dimmed, and on the alert to conjure

up the phantoms of history and make them live again. And in his literary work, therefore, ideas connected with nature or God are mere scenic effects, so to speak, having no absorbing worth in themselves, while Landor's claim to an artistic representation of life is restricted to the reflective exhibition of certain types of character.

Contrary to the habit of the humanists, who portray the manners and intellectual and moral culture distinctive of their day, Landor was in no respect an embodiment of the spirit of his time. Can we imagine what would have been the development of Oliver Goldsmith's genius apart from its eighteenth-century environment? At mention of the *Vicar of Wakefield*, or *She Stoops to Conquer*, the prudery and affectation of the women, the animality of the men, even the exaggerated

style of dressing,—all the details of
"our age of prose and reason," do
they not come to mind at once? But
Shakspeare, who penetrated the personality of Cæsar or Brutus, of Lear
or Macbeth, as profoundly as he did
that of a contemporary, who so understood the controlling forces of
human nature, as that their manifestation in any particular age and
person became an open secret to him
—even Shakspeare is far more the
mere Elizabethan writer than is Landor the mere Victorian. Recent
peculiar phases of English life were
much better known to Dickens or
Anthony Trollope than to Landor.
The power of the latter consists, not
in his grasp upon the transient aspects of character, those aspects
which a shifting environment will
transform, but upon the simpler and
more ultimate passions of the human
heart. Landor's work does not show

the careful scientific scrutiny of local types that is manifest on almost every page of Thackeray or George Eliot. The intense psychologic analysis of a George Eliot is beyond Landor's range. His psychology is more like that of Sophocles or Cicero. His representations are statuesque rather than pictorial.

If Landor does not exhibit his men and women after the pattern of the times, neither does he array himself for or against what may be regarded as the tendencies of his age. About the great scientific movement—which has, however, only recently given us its philosophic fruitage in the works of Herbert Spencer—Landor remained profoundly unconcerned. Neither Forster's *Life* nor any of Landor's writings gives us the impression that scientific questions possessed his attention in the least. And indeed, Forster, quoting from

Seymour Kirkup, says, that in conversational encounters with Francis Hare, Landor avoided the sciences. And Landor himself, in his published letter to Emerson, correcting an apparent misconception, declares that he does not despise entomology, but is only ignorant of it; as, indeed, he is of almost all science; and while he loves flowers and plants, he knows less about them than is known by a beetle or butterfly. We do not of course fall into the anachronism of expecting Landor, who died in 1864, to be affected by the Darwinian theory, since the *Origin of Species* was not published till 1859; but we should have expected a man of his positive temper to have been stirred to indignant protest against the over-estimation of material comforts, of the mechanical improvements which science has given us, and the under-estimation of the needs of the spirit.

Perhaps Landor's somewhat isolated life in Italy and Bath hindered him from perceiving how the classicism which he so cherished was threatened by the incursion of Professor Huxley and the other dragoons of natural science and " the practical." It is not to Landor, but to Ruskin or Matthew Arnold, that we must go for a defence of the humanism which alone can satisfy " our sense for beauty " and " our sense for conduct."

It is possible to inquire too curiously into psychical phenomena ; yet we venture the supposition that the sentiment of wonder, which awakens scientific aptitude, never existed in large measure in Landor's mental make-up. Wonder is the expression of a want, and is ever asking the why of things. It is the instinct for causes. Now, Landor's genius, as we hope to show more fully later, is essentially static, rather than dynamic. His style is not progressive and cumulative. He has slight ability for story-telling or for elaborate argument. Landor's power comes not from wonder, but from admiration, which rests upon a beautiful form, contented, and seeks no farther. We are not much surprised, therefore, when we find him taking no part in scientific discussion; since his genius is predominantly æsthetic and imaginative.

Nor can Landor be said to have assumed the attitude of partisan in the heated controversy between the empiricist and the intuitionalist,—a controversy which, avowed or unavowed, comprehends so much of the higher literature of the century. Who has been more strident in his vociferations against "the philosophy of dirt," and who has more manfully proclaimed Duty to be "the stern daughter of the voice of God," than Thomas Carlyle! Landor, on the other hand, in so far as he formulated his ideas, gravitated towards the utilitarian side. "This is philosophy, to make remote things tangible, common things extensively useful, useful things extensively common, and to leave the least necessary for the last. . . . Truth is not reasonably the main and ultimate object of philosophy; philosophy should seek truth merely as the means of acquiring and propagating happiness." In a letter to Southey, he says: "To increase the sum of happiness and to diminish the sum of misery, is the only right aim both of reason and of religion." Although Landor desired to walk with Epicurus on the right hand, and Epictetus on the left, he practically made life's journey with only an indulgent Epicurus; for he never was able, and indeed he never made much

serious effort, to control the impulse
of the moment. Landor's philosophic ideal, therefore, in the matter
of conduct, does not run parallel with
the modern one, as embodied in Kant
or Fichte. Kant's ideal is duty done
in the presence of inward hindrances,
of opposing impulses; Landor's ideal
is characteristically Greek. Denying
the need of conflict between man's
lower and his higher nature, it insists
upon the deep-rooted harmony of
duty and desire, and practically yields
the reins to inclination. Nowhere in
literature is a refined type of Epicureanism more persuasively set forth
than in the dialogue between Epicurus, Leontion, and Ternissa. The
Greek conception of the harmonious
play of soul and body, of mental and
material forces, is here seen in its
irresistible charm. No restless striving to impress a sense of our capa-
bilities upon others, no amount of

self-exhibition, can stand in place of that ideal which is characterized by the quiet efflorescence of what is noblest, purest, and best in each of us. This, in its highest terms, is Landor's theory of life. Indeed, if he had had a stronger hold upon intuitive truths, his standpoint might have approached very near to that of the Græco-Puritan Emerson ; and one does not wonder that the latter had studied with delight the dialogues of Landor before his memorable visit to the Villa Gherardescha, which is recorded in the *English Traits*.

Nor does Landor express the other distinctive feature of his time —its scepticism. His was not "the spirit that denies." To parade a shallow agnosticism would have met Landor's contemptuous disapproval. And surely, if Professor Huxley is speaking with accuracy when he contends that agnosticism is merely a method and not a confession of faith, or rather of doubt, he need give himself no airs for having brought such a method to light, for his mental attitude is nothing other than the characteristic one of every modern investigator. It is merely the *de omnibus dubito* of Descartes, the basal idea of modern thinking. It, however, is only a callow scepticism that would require all conviction to be grounded upon logic, would apotheosize a part of man's soul, his reasoning faculty—not recognizing him as a spiritual unit, with the power, among others, of intuitive belief. Landor, however, did not take this negative position, but was fundamentally a Comtean in religious matters. The speculative side of Christianity he placed no emphasis upon; and the decline of faith could have excited in him no such lyrical laments as it did in Matthew Arnold. Landor approached religion just as he approached all sides of life, from the individualistic standpoint. He never wearies in his dialogues of emphasizing the antithesis between the morality of states or sects and the sayings of Christ. And while his emotions did not penetrate the divine meaning of humility and self-renunciation, and his experience was foreign to such influences, he never, on the other hand, made the mistake of supposing that the strength of Christianity lay in a Hellenic Judaism, which sees a dogmatic content in the simplest moral precept of our Lord. The dialogues between Middleton and Magliabecchi, Timotheus and Lucian, Melancthon and Calvin, though not taking fairly into account the impossibility of divorcing practice from its source—theory,

2

show, nevertheless, Landor's firm grasp upon this idea, that Christianity, as he makes Romilly say in another dialogue, "lies not in belief, but in action." And Melancthon fitly closes his discussion with Calvin by declaring that " there is nothing on earth divine besides humanity."

One is tempted to draw an analogy here between Landor and Goethe. German was the only world literature that always remained a closed door to him. And when we recall the abstractness of thought, the pomposity of style, the mystical romanticism of our Teutonic neighbors, we feel that Landor, the classicist, missed less by his inability to read this language than most other men of as large mental calibre. After an inadequate acquaintance with Goethe, Landor, in his usual categorical fashion, pronounced himself disgusted with " the corrugated spicery of metaphysics," which he was pleased to find in the writings of the great German. Nevertheless, these two men had points in common. One side of Goethe's nature was Greek, the other side intensely modern. Landor in one aspect resembled the Greek, in the other the Roman. They met, therefore, on common Hellenic ground. Goethe ⌐ looked at things from the critic's standpoint. He lightly disengaged himself from the object, and then with perfect self-poise studied its effectiveness. Landor, for all his Hellenism, could rarely become so disinterested ; the active ethical impulse was ever and again pulling at his heart-strings. It is not, however, our purpose to draw out these lines of community or difference, but simply to quote a passage from Goethe which gives expression to a positivism

similar to Landor's. Goethe says:
" But an able man, who has something
to do here, and must toil and strive
day by day to accomplish it, leaves
the future world till it comes, and
contents himself with being active
and useful in this."   Nevertheless,
Goethe's positivism, unlike Landor's,
is occasionally lighted up by flashes
of insight into the very life of things,
as in the Prologue in Heaven in
Faust, an allegory infinite in its
suggestiveness.

It is evident from what has been
said that Landor cannot be represented as one of the mouth-pieces of
his time, since he was not coerced
by the logic of contemporary events
to the choice of standpoints coinci-
dent with those of his fellow-think-
ers, but when he took such similar
positions was constrained by the
necessity of his own temperament
rather than by external influences.

In other words, Landor was an idealist whose intellectual life lay in the past.

It might be contended, however, that in his literary criticism and his political writings Landor's interests are plainly concerned with the present, and that he is here unquestionably the child of his age. This is only partially true. It is conceded that much of Landor's criticism is devoted to his contemporaries, and is largely appreciative. In one of the *Imaginary Conversations*, Southey and Porson discuss with much discrimination the merits and defects of Wordsworth's poetry, and pass in review the Laodamia, whose classic restraint naturally appealed to a lover of Homer and Æschylus. Landor is even catholic enough to admire writers so at variance from his own standard as Dickens and Robert Browning. Nevertheless, the large

prerogatives which criticism has assumed in this age were not at all well
understood by him.   He sometimes
deals hard blows against the *Edin-
burgh* and *Quarterly Reviews*, yet
his own criticism is not always essentially different from Lord Jef-
frey's or Gifford's. Landor was fond
of impressing his "whim upon the
immutable past," and his hot-headed
admiration or repugnance frequently
disabled him from striking that careful balance which is necessary to
sane literary judgments.   Indeed
his estimates rarely appear to be
thoroughly reasoned. They concern
themselves almost   entirely with
qualities of style, and do not penetrate the personality of the author
and grasp his relation to his period.
As Mr. John Morley admirably puts
it: " Minor verse-writers may fairly
be consigned, without disrespect, to
the region of the literature of taste ;

and criticism of their work takes the shape of a discussion of stray graces, of new turns of thought, of little variations of shade and color, of their conformity to the accepted rules that constitute the technique of poetry. The loftier masters . . . besides these precious gifts, come to us with the size and quality of great historic forces, for they represent the hopes and energies, the dreams and the consummation of the human intelligence in its most enormous movements." Every important writer, therefore, is the delegate of a vast intellectual and moral constituency, for whose needs he seeks to legislate. Landor himself never was, nor sought to be, such a social force; and he did not view other writers under this aspect. While Carlyle and later critics have entered into deep sympathy with Dante, regarding him as the efflorescence of scholasticism and chivalry, Landor studied the great Florentine as an isolated phenomenon, and thus lost the sense of historic perspective.

Nor does Landor exhibit that close psychologic and philosophical insight which great critics, like Coleridge and Amiel, possess. Landor's criticism makes slight endeavor to seize upon an author's philosophy of life and his organizing ideas, and fails to trace the obscure links between the personality of a writer and his literary contributions. Authors are not mere logic machines. Landor himself has beautifully said: "The heart is the creator of the poetical world; only the atmosphere is from the brain." Hence the business of the critic is to examine the emotive and ethical impulses that lie at the root of the intellectual life. For this kind of penetrative, sympathetic criticism, Landor had few talents. His judgments, on the other hand, consist in a somewhat arbitrary assertion, generally couched in exquisite imagery, of one writer's superiority over another. Now, nothing is easier, and, I may add, nothing is more inconclusive than for a critic to insist upon arranging his victims according to his own ready-made, graduated scale of excellence. This defect is not rare even among critics of note. Not only Landor, but Arnold, in his reasoned dogmatism, and Swinburne, in his intuitional dogmatism, are too prone to set up their own personal estimate of the rank of an author as the supreme tribunal from which there is no appeal. Whereas, it must be apparent that whether one shall assert Thackeray to be a greater novelist than Dickens, or George Eliot's *Middlemarch* a finer novel than Mrs. Ward's

Robert Elsmere, will depend largely upon temperament, not to speak of other causes: and since none of us can boast the possession of an ideal temperament, with faculties ideally adjusted and harmonized; in the midst of the many possible criteria, both intellectual and æsthetic, it becomes the part of wisdom and humility quietly to justify the faith that is in us, so to speak, without representing our faith as the measure of the credible. Arnold's exaggerated valuation of Byron, Swinburne's of Victor Hugo, and Landor's of his friend and coadjutor, Southey, are to be classed, therefore, as deflections from tactful, well-reasoned criticism. The last mentioned preference reminds us, perhaps unjustly, of Dr. Johnson's remark, that "the reciprocal civility of authors is one of the most risible scenes in the farce of life."

Now, although we dare not retract any of these strictures upon Landor's critical power, yet we would be confessing ourselves deficient in this faculty did we not acknowledge his invariably fine perception on the formal side of literature. Landor's catholic range of reading, and his born instinct for expression enabled him—as we shall have frequent occasion to note in treating of his own style—to appraise the literary qualities of many authors both ancient and modern, with much æsthetic *finesse* and in terms that, in their way, are final. Nevertheless, just as we would not suppose ourselves to have exhausted a good painting, when we had estimated the effects of perspective, light and shade, tone and gradation, and the other technicalities, but would seek above all to enter into the emotional life of the artist, and to extract the idea of the picture ; so we cannot pluck out the heart of the mystery in a work of prose or poetry by directing our critical scalpels merely to the more or less superficial phenomena of form, but must also question an author as to his organizing ideas. It is true, however, that matter and form, idea and execution, are so fused that the formal element is never wholly superficial. An affected style is just as really a negative index of thought and character as are the positive indices, simplicity and sincerity. Hence, the critic who discriminates nicely the forms of things may be in a fair way to appreciate the things themselves.

The final plea that might be made in behalf of Landor as a social force, and as illustrative of his age, would be drawn from his political compositions. Born at the beginning of the American Revolution, and dying near the close of our Civil War, and all through his life feeling an intense sympathy in English and Continental politics, Landor would seem to be peculiarly fitted to take a comprehensive and disinterested view of European polity. It remains true, however, that his political diatribes and conversations are the least balanced, the most ephemeral, of his productions. In many of them, this fact might be ascribed to the necessity of the case; since even a spirited refutation of some partisan measure, arising from the exigency of the moment, could not be expected to have enough permanent applicability to keep it alive amid the fading circumstances which it celebrated. This explanation, however, is not sufficient. The main fault lay in Landor's unbridled enthusiasm, and his inability to make careful inductions. Aroused by an exalted longing for liberty and justice, Landor lost all power of discrimination. Every Pole or Italian or Greek who fought for freedom was an angel of light, and all their opponents were angels of darkness. Proceeding upon this postulate, Landor indulges in rhetoric, idealistic and grandiose. At times there is a resonance in his periods equal to the most dignified utterances of Cicero. Yet because of his impatient contempt for considerations of expediency or compromise, because of his hot-headed political idealism, he usually fails so to grasp the situation as to make his appeals tell. Perhaps if he had entertained somewhat more regard for the man of statecraft, and had tried, now and then, to take the politician's point of view, his pleas might have possessed more weight.

As it was, Landor cannot be called a normal citizen. His social rela-

tionships were of the most varied
and delightful sort, but his political
ties were virtually non-existent—except when he got into one of his nu-
merous squabbles with the Italian
police or with some other officials at
home or abroad.   True, while at
Llanthony, he sought to obtain a
magistracy ; and how like an outraged Roman did he behave when
for some petty reason it was refused
him.   Yet all through his life, subsequent to his youthful experience
as a disciple of that whimsical old
pedant and politician, Dr. Parr, Landor held himself aloof from practical
politics, and even boasted, after the
manner of Thoreau, that he had
never entered a club, and never cast
a vote.   Knowing this, we sometimes
grow impatient with his oft-repeated
tirades against the politician, and
his dogmatic insistance on the superiority of the man of letters.   We

feel at such times that Landor prefers heat to light.

Holding the idea of war in noble detestation, Landor was wont to insist, with much show of seriousness, upon the justifiability of tyrannicide. And he makes Demosthenes say, characteristically : " Rapine and licentiousness are the precursors and followers of even the most righteous war. A single blow against the worst of mortals may prevent them. Many years and much treasure are usually required for an uncertain issue, besides the stagnation of traffic the prostration of industry, the innumerable maladies arising from towns besieged, and regions depopulated. A moment is sufficient to avert all these calamities. No usurper, no invader, should be permitted to exist on earth." Nothing could illustrate better than this Landor's emphatic recognition of the power inherent in chosen individuals. With a sublime disregard of what we now call the force of heredity and environment,—comprehending in this phrase social custom and individual habit, and sentiments which outlive the ideas producing them, all those subtle and manifold causes, mental and material, which superimpose their weight upon personality, — Landor seems to look upon men and things as pawns which a tyrant can dispose of according to his whim. This individualistic idealism, which could slur over whole series of causes, rendered him incapable of entering into the inner life of history, as it is seen in the action of masses of men. Thus, for example, the philosophic aspect of that greatest of all cataclysms, the French Revolution, was without its full *rationale* to Landor's mind. That the streams of tendency which proceeded from the

3

Aufklärung,—from the Encyclopæ-
dists, from Rousseau, and the rest,—
uniting with the pent-up emotions
of a people downtrodden by priest
and noble, but at last awakened to a
sense of their prerogatives, should
flow on with ever-accelerated speed
to the horrors of 1792, was certainly
a spectacle calculated to excite the
intense interest of all on-lookers.
Yet we do not find Landor following
the drama with the intelligent sympathy of Wordsworth or Coleridge.
There is a germ of truth in Carlyle's
saying, reported by Emerson, that
" Landor's principle was mere rebel-
lion." Relative to this time, Forster
says of him : " He reasoned little,
but his instincts were all against
authority, or what took to him the
form of its abuse." Thus he sided
with the French Republic, but he
did so without an adequate insight
into the causes from which it

sprang or the direction in which it tended.

In several ways a parallel might be drawn between the political principles of Landor and those of Milton. Both were iconoclasts ; both were apostles of the idea, but while Milton's *a priori* reasoning was the natural outcome of his age, Landor's was opposed to the inductive spirit, which is ever growing stronger and more effective ; both longed for the time when the few virtuous and wise would bear rule, yet without creating any definite constructive scheme by which their hopes might be realized. Both must take a second rank as political thinkers,—though Milton, of course, stands far above Landor, —because both failed so to ground their aspirations upon sound precedent and present conditions as that a rejuvenescent future could, by their efforts, grow out of the past, as the flower from its stalk. Both abhorred a many-headed Demos, where, instead of one tyrant, there are thousands. Indeed Landor could never bring himself to stomach our own republican institutions, regarding them in somewhat the same light as did Matthew Arnold. Landor loved the distinction and charm which emanate from a true nobility; and while he also loved the people he loved them as some of us do—at a dignified distance.

But it may suddenly be asked: "If all this is true of Landor; if he neither portrays the life of his age, nor represents its tendencies, and if, even in those occupations where he attempted to affect his generation, in criticism and political pamphlet, he does not vitally affect it, just what is his claim upon the lover of literature and of life?" If the converse of Spinoza's famous dictum be true, if all negation be determination, as it undoubtedly is, then our efforts at estimating Landor by a process of exclusion have not been valueless. Notwithstanding, it is high time to give some positive reasons for regarding him as a master in the field of thought and expression ; and this we can now do with a clear conscience and without reservations.

Landor was, in its most exclusive sense, a literary man. Unlike so many in our own day he made no serious attempt, except it might be in his pleas for spelling reform, to combine literature with any kind of propagandism, philosophical, scientific, religious, or ethical. He came near to trying this in his political writings ; but, as we saw, he was there ineffective. Furthermore, Landor was a deep student and portrayer of the past. But we prefer not to place too much emphasis upon his classical and pagan cast of mind ; because we regard such catch-words as inexact and misleading. Landor was a member of no sect which might wave its classical or romantic banner. And if he was at home in ancient Greece, he was also acclimated to the Italy of Petrarch and Boccaccio, and the England of Shakspeare or of Cromwell. In nothing is he more distinctive than in his haughty independence of mere models. Like the artist of the early Renaissance, nature was his teacher, and he knew no other. This fact constitutes one of his claims upon our consideration ; for any man who can look upon the drama of life about him, and into his own soul, and then tell what he sees, will always afford the needed spectacles for our purblind eyes. Landor was, as Mrs. Browning well said, "most Greek, because most English"; since it is not he who mimics the Greeks, but

he who does as the Greeks did,
namely, follows nature—he it is who
possesses their spirit. Therefore, it
is not as an antiquarian that we
would eulogize Landor. Indeed,
when he plays this rôle, he is rarely
successful; for his scholarship was
not of that infinitely painstaking
sort which requires everything, down
to the lacing of a sandal, to conform
to the original. Landor listened to
the men and women around him, he
listened to the beatings of his own
sympathetic heart; and then, with
these tones still ringing in his soul,
he shut his eyes; and lo, long processions of the good, the great, and
the unfortunate of former days filed
before him; he watched their pensive
gestures, he caught their calm reflections or their impassioned replies;
and straightway he chiselled and
polished the fast vanishing scene
in statuesque verse or monumental

prose. Landor, therefore, fixed his gaze neither upon a model nor an audience, but upon the object itself. Such a consecrated ideal of authorship will always, as it did in Landor's case, bear its measure of fruit.

One of the ways of appreciating Landor's works is to approach them through the medium of his personality. As a man he was as unique as Oliver Goldsmith or Dr. Johnson. In outward appearance he stood for the prince and lion among men—his face showing great force and aggressiveness, with high arched brow, strongly moulded nose, and a mouth whose downward curving lines suggest a passionate and even caustic nature. Yet, in the presence of his friends, and especially of ladies, this face could beam with a wealth of old-world grace and courtesy, his whole demeanor bespeaking that

dignity and deference which the rapid
intercourse of our later day rarely
takes time for. His actions, his biographers tell us, were a trifle awkward
—not, of course, from ill-breeding,
but from the aimlessness of the unpractical man. And, indeed, in its
way, we may imagine that this fact
made his manners all the more attractive. In his not infrequent fits
of ungovernable passion, it is said
that his thumbs were not clinched,
but relaxed, this seeming to indicate
that his rage was louder than it was
deep, that it was a habit of speech
and gesture rather than the dethrone-
ment of personality, and the entire
subordination of will to animal impulse. In other words, it is probable
that Landor never completely lost
himself in these wild exhibitions of
temper,—that he never completely
sacrificed his freedom to a mere
brutish determinism. While the

surface of his soul was in turmoil the depths lay undisturbed.

Too much emphasis has been placed upon Landor's impetuous, ungovernable temperament by his critics. To insist upon this side of his character is to view him superficially. It is as though one should put special stress upon Sir Walter Scott's lameness, or Charles Lamb's propensity to stammer. Landor's pride and anger never penetrated into the sanctuary of his soul-life, and profaned his better nature. They were merely uproarious protestations against an ungenial environment. And in almost every case, if the motives which animated his wild outbreaks should be examined, they would be found noble, though misapplied. Possessed of a just regard for his dignity and high desert, he was all aflame at the suspicion of a slight. Thus there is something

amusing, if it were not so pathetic, in Landor's majestic letter to Lord Normanby, in retort upon this English minister's cold reception of him at the Cascine, in the presence of "innumerable Florentines." This was in Landor's old age, after his generosity and gallant attentions to a young girl at Bath had been shamefully misrepresented ; and he, having resorted to his old childish weapons of satiric verse, had been obliged to pay a heavy fine, and had left his native country, sorrow-stricken yet unconquered. The letter closes with these majestic words : " We are both of us old men, my lord, and are verging on decrepitude and imbecility, else my note might be more energetic. I am not inobservant of distinctions. You by the favor of a minister are the Marquis of Normanby, I by the grace of God am
   " WALTER SAVAGE LANDOR."

Indeed, the six years that Landor lived after the Bath scandal are so filled with pathetic material that his indiscretions of former days are forgotten in our indignation at the exasperating treatment which "the old lion" received, even at the hands of his own family, and in our admiration for the general nobility of his aims. And it must be borne in mind that Landor's wrath was aroused by an affront or insult done to others as effectually as though it had been done to himself. His anger was a perversion of a noble attribute— an unbending, though not always accurate, sense of justice. Therefore, if Professor Dowden means to convey a weighty observation, when he remarks that the first thing one is tempted to say of Landor is, that he was emphatically "an uncivilized man," he is giving by no means a fair impression of our author's

character.   Landor was, like Carlyle or Emerson, or other great personages, somewhat of an aboriginal
man.   It was inherent in his nature
to make unique estimates. He never
sought to drain the currents of his
thought into established channels,
but preferred above all things to
place his own independent construction upon the facts of the universe.
This construction, however, was not
always the sound product of reflection.   Too often it was the result of
unreasoning prejudice, of likes and
dislikes canonized by mere dint of
repetition. Nevertheless, even these
ideas have their interest as proceeding from a massive and original personality.   While ordinary men dress,
think, and act after the pattern of
their day, extraordinary men create
a taste rather than conform to one.
From the common man's standpoint
Landor was certainly uncivilized.

He was uncivilized in his flaring bursts of anger. But his passion was not a fire smouldering unsuspected beneath the ashes. It was the sudden response of a proud and, withal, a gracious nature. Therefore, to apply the word uncivilized to one of Landor's exquisite refinement and delicacy ; to him whose princely politeness, even such a connoisseur as Lady Blessington signalized, and whose representations of women, and of all that is beautiful and suave, have been surpassed neither by ancient nor modern,—is ill-timed as well as inaccurate.

Landor was, as we have intimated, a man, generous, ardent, and sincere. We do not therefore propose to go over the tiresome list of his misunderstandings and quarrels with fellow-students, teachers, father, wife, friends, publishers, and civil officials. His biographers give us little more than the bare facts in the case; the mitigating circumstances and explanations we are usually left to infer as best we may. We must judge Landor by his high ideal of dignified and gracious conduct rather than by his performance, which may have been ludicrously undignified. Viewed from a somewhat external and unsympathetic standpoint, the world is hopelessly vulgar. It seems to care so little for intellectual pursuits. It lives in an atmosphere where ideas look so hazy, and gold is more dazzling than the sun. It is only natural, therefore, that an unpractical idealist like Landor should have found the world a place hard to breathe in. He preferred to walk "alone on the far eastern uplands, meditating and remembering." He even goes so far as to write to Lady Blessington: "Most things are real to me, except realities." And indeed, Landor seems to have let the reality of family ties hang about him but loosely. Thus, in the spring of 1835 he could leave his fair Italian home, his wife and children, without apparently any violent wrench with the past, and without any excruciating compunctions, because, forsooth, his wife's temper did not quite tally with his own proud, commanding ways. For years afterward he could lead an independent life at Bath, not allowing the thought of his duty as husband and father to interrupt an agreeable social intercourse or a pleasant trend of meditation. And after grief had passed "into near Memory's more quiet shade," he could say good-bye to Italy in this impersonal manner:

"I leave thee, beauteous Italy! no more
　From the high terraces, at even-tide,
　To look supine into thy depths of sky,

Thy golden moon between the cliff
    and me,
Or thy dark spires of fretted cypresses
Bordering the channel of the milky
    way."

While one cannot but feel the charm of these lines, as a natural description, it were well if they had been *ethicalized*, so to speak, by a few regrets at parting from wife and children, by a few compunctions at severing the most responsible and enduring of ties. But Landor, unlike most persons, does not appear to have minded these sudden breaks in his existence. All that he required was an ideal or imaginative continuity of life. If he only had the worthies of former days that he might glory in their deeds and weep over their sufferings, he was content. In examining such a character, it is therefore more profitable to ask how he realized himself in his writings

4

than how he failed to realize himself in the exasperating concerns of daily life. Of Landor, as indeed of most authors, it is manifest that his books are his truest self.

A first word to be said of Landor as a literary man is, that he was unswervingly original. He represented the Independent in the Republic of Letters. He was an avowed enemy to the prevailing habit of quotation, and he stoutly refused to put into the mouth of his speakers any sentiments that history might have ascribed to them. He sought by his fine historic imagination to catch and portray real men, not their mannerisms. This proud independent spirit was the source of his strength and of his weakness. On the one hand, it led him to uphold the dignity and disinterestedness of literature, and to aim above all things at satisfying his own exacting sense for literary form. On the other hand, it brought him into conflict with his audience. There is a just mean between the low men-pleaser and the literary aristocrat. And this mean Landor never took the pains to strike. He is either unsympathetic with his readers, or else oblivious of them. Therefore he sometimes leaves his meaning needlessly opaque. His ideal, comprehending a classic severity and restraint of speech, he makes no effort to supply his audience with necessary sequences and comfortable transitions. He sometimes cuts away the ground, so that it requires an agile imagination to take the leap from point to point. This fact goes some way toward accounting for Landor's unpopularity, the reasons for which have been discussed by his critics *ad nauseam.* And relevant to this discussion we may remark, that, to judge from recent attractive editions of the *Imaginary Conversations*, the *Examination of Shakspeare*, and the *Pericles and Aspasia*, what has been satirized as Landor's "late-dinner theory" bids fair to be realized, notwithstanding the head-shakings of dubious critics.

Landor's high ideal of authorship is seen in his manner of writing. His carefulness showed itself, not so much in his collection of materials, as in his efforts after adequacy of expression. For his facts he depended upon a tenacious memory, which could open at will the vast storehouse of his reading and reflection. Landor's library, at any one time, was small. Actuated by an inveterate generosity, he mastered a book and then gave it away. But notwithstanding this lack, he could write letters between *Pericles and Aspasia* which are so fraught with Hellenic grace and beauty, even down to the merest detail, that only a lifeless antiquary would be so irrelevant as to insist upon historic inaccuracies. And in regard to style, that man must indeed be a master in the art of literary expression who would pick serious flaws in Landor's workmanship. This perfection of form sprang partly from a gift, and partly from a faculty for taking pains. Landor used to compose in the open air, surrounded by the flowers and dumb creatures, which he looked upon as humble companions. Here his sympathetic, fibrous voice might be heard repeating and testing his sentences, until they became as beautifully modulated as a cathedral organ in the hands of a master musician. His whole soul was in his work, and he was deeply sincere when he said : "I hate false words, and seek with care, difficulty, and moroseness those that fit the thing." He could not divert his imagination from the particular subject under way, and was at a loss to conceive how Southey was able to compose two poems at one time. "When I write a poem, my heart and all my feelings are upon it. I never commit adultery with another, and high poems will not admit flirtation." It is indeed hard to find the literary conscience as fully developed as it was in Landor. There is, however, at least one other instance on record,—that of the French novelist Flaubert, who was almost a fanatic on style, and used to exclaim in thunderous tones: "No, the only important and enduring thing under the sun, is a well formed sentence, a sentence with hand and foot, that harmonizes with the sentences preceding and following it, and that falls pleasantly on the ear when it is read." And Flaubert, they say, would relentlessly pursue a repeated word, even at the distance of thirty or forty lines, and so much as the recurrence of the same syllable in the same sentence annoyed him. Sometimes, becoming dissatisfied with a single letter, he would spare no pains till he had lighted upon a substitute word. Such struggles to attain perfection remind one of the all-night agony that Landor experienced, when he thought he had been guilty of a false quantity, in making the first vowel of the word *flagrans* short, in one of his Latin poems, which he had just before sent off for publication.

These efforts, as we have intimated, were not in vain. The texture of Landor's style represents an exquisite blending of diversified materials. And though there may be rents now and then in the thought, there are at least no visible patches in the expression. Moreover, the style is an admirable exposition of the man himself, its primary qualities being rightly of an ethical rather than of a purely intellectual cast. While at times Landor condescends to sculpture his sentences in a winning, graceful, Praxitelean way, he is in the main characteristically epic, his periods possessing the dignity and massiveness of Phidian marbles. By epic, I refer to his grand compendious manner, and would not be understood to imply that our author has that "divine fluidity of movement," which Matthew Arnold finds to be so characteristic of Homer and Chaucer. Indeed, it is just the absence of this, that one notices in Landor's prose, which is not progressive, but is rather a series of sentences organically related, yet at the same time semi-detached, each standing out in bold relief. This peculiarity is what we would call the static quality of Landor's prose. And we by no means criticise his workmanship because it possesses this quality to such a high degree ; since, for the utterance of solid reflections upon human nature, this is the ideal style—a style where the sentences are made up of semi-independent clauses, and where all is eminently direct, simple, and urbane.

But when this dignified and somewhat sententious manner is made the vehicle for writing of a dramatic rather than a reflective cast, there results a species of classicism, which Landor's dialogues of action splendidly exhibit. And as the word classic is frequently used in a vague, indiscriminate way, it is well to mark that this peculiarity, namely, the expression of impassioned thought in terms of strict grammatical sobriety, is one of the several features of the classicist. Unwilling to contort his style or to sacrifice ideal excellence to a crude realism, Landor was careful that his personages should maintain a certain degree of regularity and precision of utterance, even in the most animated dialogues. And as all true art is a spiritual interpretation of nature and the human soul, and is selective, and therefore above reality, he was justified in the result. In this respect Landor somewhat resembles Nathaniel Hawthorne, who, as Mr. Lathrop says, " could scarcely permit his actors to speak loosely or ungrammatically."

But after the knife of criticism has done its best to dissect the charm of a style like Landor's, the essence of its beauty, so volatile and yet so real, has vanished; and we must be content to admire even if we cannot fully formulate our admiration. Suffice it to say, that Landor's wonderful style, taken in connection with the

delicate aphorisms, the weighty reflections, and the noble and beautiful
scenes from the drama of human life
—which he has given us in the books
we are about to examine more particularly,—is enough to secure him
a permanent place in literature. A
very few writers, like Aristotle, live
by sheer force of thought ; the vast
majority live by the force of a fine
style in vital union with fine thought.
Landor belongs to this latter class.

II.

LANDOR'S POETRY.

LANDOR'S POETRY.

THOUGH Landor was wont to refer to verse as his pastime, and prose as his occupation, still the quality of much of his poetry is high enough to merit an appreciative recognition. Brought up according to the English school system, which trains the youth to acquire a facility in scribbling Latin verses, Landor, as was natural, took so readily to the translation of Greek and Roman themes into rhymed pentameters, that by his twentieth year he had gotten out his first volume of English and Latin poems, some satiric, others descriptive. What especially strikes one in the selections which Forster has preserved of these verses is their conventional manner.

" So, when Medea, on her native strand,
Beheld the *Argo* lessen from the land ;
The tender pledges of her love she
    bore,
Frantic, and raised them high above
    the shore.
' Thus, thus may Jason, faithless as
    he flies,
Faithless and heedless of Medea's
    cries,
Behold his babes, oppose the adverse
    gales,
Return to Colchis those retiring
    sails.' "

This is the artificial sing-song of Pope's muse.

Yet by his twenty-third year Landor had brought out another poem *Gebir*, whose massive blank verse is as far removed from Pope as is the *Paradise Lost* from the *Essay on Man*. The advance is remarkable. Yet we do not agree with Forster in ascribing it to the effect of making translations. We would rather say that the efficient cause was Landor's careful and enthusiastic study of Milton. Some time after his rustication from Oxford, Landor settled in a wild secluded spot of Wales. And here he fell in with Pindar, whose "proud complacency and scornful strength" he particularly noted, and whose poetry he resolved to imitate, at least as respects its weighty brevity and exclusiveness. Here, also, he used to declaim, with glowing admiration, the magnificent lines of *Paradise Lost*, and at last came to think that even the great hexameter sounded tinkling when he had recited aloud, in his solitary walks on the seashore, the haughty appeal of Satan and the repentance

5

of Eve.   It is, then, to the influence of our greatest master in the grand style that we would find Landor most indebted for the many fine qualities contained in the verse of *Gebir*.

Before estimating the value of this poem, it is only just that we should make a general remark upon Landor as a poet—a remark which must tend irrevocably to fix his place in the choir of the muses. Unlike the genius of the great original bards, Landor's poetic talent does not seem to have sprung from an irresistible necessity of his soul towards self-expression.   Nor does his poetry appear to have developed naturally from within outward, from the early lyric outpourings of a solitary soul to the later dramatic and epic representations, when the mind has grown more familiar with the world around it.   On the contrary,

Landor's first two considerable poems were an epic and a tragedy; his later poetry was in the main pastoral or erotic. This development, or perhaps lack of development, is the reverse of the normal growth of a poet's mind, as is seen in Shakspeare or Milton, and suggests that Landor never felt the poetic impulse as a sacred and irresistible mission. He says in *Gebir* that there was aroused within him " the feverish thirst of song "; but we believe that poetry was not to him, as it is to one inevitably a poet, the very water of life. Indeed, his reference to versification as a pastime would of itself confirm this view.

Nevertheless, *Gebir*, his first long poem, is remarkable both for the vivid force of imagination displayed, and for the full tones of its blank verse. As a whole, the poem is a magnificent failure, the different parts being blocked together so abruptly that it is wellnigh impossible, without explanations, to get a satisfactory conception of the *ensemble*. Landor's admiration for Pindar, and his consequent desire to be " as compendious and exclusive," led him to cart off so many loads from *Gebir* (as he expressed it) that the transitions in the plot are not easy to follow.

Moreover, the plot itself, which he took from a tale purporting to be Arabian, and which has for its idea to reprimand pride of conquest, is somewhat grotesque and improbable. Landor thought he saw in it *magnificum quid sub crepusculo antiquitatis ;* but at least he did not succeed in adequately conveying this quality. Indeed the parts that deal with the twilighted region, where the natural and the supernal converge are, to our mind at least, the weakest in the poem. Landor's real strength in poetry, as he himself must have seen later, lay in a clear, chaste, objective rendering of the sunny, idyllic life which we are accustomed to associate with the Greeks, and which Theocritus, Bion, and Moschus have rendered immortally attractive and beautiful. And his most characteristic ideal, expressed in the poetic prose by which Mr. J. A. Symonds describes Greek life, was a feast of " perpetual sunshine and perpetual ease—no work from year to year that might degrade the body or impair the mind, no dread of hell, no yearning after heaven, but summer-time of youth and autumn of old age, and loveless death be-wept and bravely borne." Landor was therefore incompetent to spiritualize and render deeply symbolic those parts of his poem which deal with the under world and with Masarian Marthyr, the sorceress. Indeed, Gebir's visit to the Shades is rendered almost ridiculous by his there encountering, despite the anachronism, the Stuarts and George III., who was ever Landor's detestation. What we miss, then, in this treatment is that air of supernatural realism, so prominent in another poem, which appeared the same year, the *Rhyme of the Ancient Mariner*. Landor is either too real and homely, as when Marthyr, after having indulged in the most outlandish scenic effects, exclaims to Dalica :

" Oh, what more pleasant than the short-
  breathed sigh,
 When, laying down your burthen at the
  gate,
 And, dizzy with long wanderings, you
  embrace
 The cool and quiet of a home-spun
  bed."

For here we find it incompatible with
our former notion of the terrible sorceress, who can shrivel in one breath
the bones of her victims, "as all the
sands we tread on could not in a thousand years," that she should condescend to the cool and quiet of a
home-spun bed. Or else, on the
other hand, Landor fails to excite
emotion, because his horrors are too
horrid to simulate probability even
for a moment. There is, therefore,
not that perfect blending of natural
and supernatural elements which
arouses our sense for the mysterious
without conflicting with our sense for
the probable.

But after these abatements have
been made, there remain passages, as
for example the loves of Gebir and
Tamar, and the nuptial morning,
which, for purity of outline, incisive
strokes, and at one time graceful
psychologic touches, at another,

strong, majestic lines, would bear comparison with portions of Keats' *Hyperion*, and would justify the warm admiration of a Shelley. Tamar's narrative of his encounter with the Nymph, for example, which contains the noted passage on the sea-shell, has all the directness and chaste restraint which is characteristic of the best Greek art. And while the picture of Charoba's nuptial morning may suggest somewhat ignobly the physical side of her passion for Gebir, yet many of the lines, notably those portraying her fears, are exquisitely handled.

As regards the technical quality of the verse, we might criticise the unpleasant iteration of syllables, sometimes in the same line, as " Saw the blood *man*tle in his *man*ly cheeks," also the tendency to awkward Latinized phraseology, as " Him overcome her serious voice bespake,"

and the too regular beat of the blank
verse ; but we prefer rather to admire
the frequent felicity, and, at times,
the grandeur of expression. The
following is worthy to stand with
the introductory lines of the second
book of *Paradise Lost*, as a splendid
specimen of the periodic sentence :

" Once a fair city, courted then by kings,
　Mistress　of　nations,　thronged　by
　　　palaces,
　Raising　her head o'er destiny, her face
　Glowing with pleasure and with palms
　　　refreshed,
　Now　pointed　at　by　Wisdom　or　by
　　　Wealth,
　Bereft of beauty, bare of ornament,
　Stood in the wilderness of woe, Masar."

This is one of the many places in
Gebir that Shelley never tired of repeating.

　But notwithstanding the admiration of a few select spirits—Shelley,

Southey, Reginald Heber, De Quincey, and perhaps Coleridge,—*Gebir* fell upon the general public a dead failure. Landor was not honored by the vituperation which Wordsworth or Keats received, yet he came in for his modest share of the uncritical lashings which the critics of his day held it their privilege to impose upon a new and original author. This by no means destroyed his self-confidence, for he never doubted his own ability, he only doubted whether others could be made to recognize it; still, applause does supplement and strengthen one's consciousness of merit and give just that final impulse which is needed to accomplish great things. Landor felt this, and wrote to Southey: " The *popularis aura*, though we are ashamed or unable to analyze it, is requisite for the health and growth of genius "; and again he wrote in his high and mighty

way : " I confess to you, if even foolish men had read *Gebir*, I should
have continued to write poetry,—
there is something of summer in the
hum of insects."

As it was, he did not long abstain
from versifying. Indeed, all through
his life he was accustomed to vow,
after some friction with public or
publishers, that he would never again
touch pen to paper ; and behold, the
very next day would find him at
work as sedulously as ever, producing a new dialogue or poem. Only
two years after the publication of
Gebir, Landor had got out a little
pamphlet of poems from the Arabic
and Persian, purporting to have
been rendered from a French translation, and garnished with elaborate
notes, which Mr. Colvin thinks were
meant to mystify the reader. These
effusions have not come down to us.
But two years subsequent to this,

there appeared *Chrysaor* and the *Phocæans*, two poems which are still preserved among Landor's collected works. The *Phocæans* is painfully obscure, an unintelligible fragment ; but *Chrysaor*, which is also in its general drift somewhat puzzling, merits more attention. It has for its subject an incident in the war between the Gods and Titans, and thus foreshadows, as has been suggested, the *Hyperion* of Keats. Indeed there are in it sounding lines and felicities of phrase which a Keats need not have been ashamed to own.

"The azure concave of their curling
    shells"

is surely not without the magic of expression which we so much admire in the author of *Lamia*, and the *Eve of St. Agnes*. And in general, we may claim for the *Chrysaor* that as a specimen of massive blank verse it is comparable with many portions of *Gebir* and *Count Julian*, partaking of the character of Landor's early grand style as distinguished from the light graceful manner of the idyllic poems, which he wrote subsequently. And Mr. Colvin goes so far as to hold that the blank verse is more varied, and therefore finer, than the regularly modulated lines of *Gebir*.

Notwithstanding this measure of accomplishment after his publication of *Gebir*, it remains true that Landor's life from 1798 to about 1810 was desultory and unproductive, this fact being perhaps partially due to the ill-success of his epic. However, in the late summer of the latter year he began a tragedy, *Count Julian*, which he completed by the beginning of the next spring. The scene of this drama is naturally laid in Spain, a country then exciting men's minds on account of the political complications which had arisen from Napoleon's infamous efforts to place his brother Joseph upon the Spanish throne—efforts which had resulted in the sudden uprising of the Spanish people. In his ardent sympathy for their resistance to the French despot, Landor had gone to Spain in 1808, offered himself as a volunteer, sent to the government ten thousand reals for the relief of the inhabitants of Venturada, a town destroyed by the French, and promised to equip and lead to the field troops up to the number of a thousand. All this speaks well for Landor's generous soul. And while his expedition was anything but a success from a military standpoint, and while, moreover, his evil genius of pride and precipitancy managed to make his experience uncomfortable by flaring up offensively at some harmless ex-

pression of Stuart, the English en-
voy ; still Landor's journey was not
devoid of results, for the knowledge
of Spain thus got enabled him to
impart a local coloring to his drama,
which, as Southey remarked in contrasting it with his own Spanish epic
of *Roderick*, gave Landor an ad-
vantage.

The semi-legendary history of
Spain appears to have excited a
strong fascination in Landor's mind ;
and by making choice of that grandly
tragic story, wherein Count Julian,
discovering that his daughter has
been outraged by King Roderick,
determines to give over his native
land to the Moors, whom he had
just before defeated, Landor was able
to construct a drama, whose characters are hewn out, naked and colossal
as the *Prometheus* of Æschylus.

By thus objectifying desperate and
tremendous emotions in imagery so

clear, pregnant, and concise that the
very words aim to be as distinct and
real as the deeds they celebrate,
Landor was following the highest
Greek models, Æschylus and Sophocles; but by reason of this very
loftiness of purpose, he must needs
pitch his theme in an ideal key, which
it was wellnigh impossible for him
to sustain without, at the same time,
drowning that modest volume of
homely human interest requisite to
the harmony and truth of the whole.
Hence, if we would justly laud a sublime picture like that which Count
Julian draws of himself, when he
stands in unutterable misery before
the ruined Roderick—

"I stand abased before insulting crime,
  I falter like a criminal myself;
  The hand that hurled thy chariot o'er
      its wheels,
  That held thy steeds erect and motion-
      less,

As molten statues on some palace gate,
Shakes as with palsied age before thee
　　now,—"

a picture which Southey declared to
be " the grandest image of power that
ever poet produced;" we must at
the same time recognize that such
passages lose much of their force,
because Landor is ever striving to
maintain a too continuous level of
sublimity.　He does not grasp the
magic power inhering in contrast.
All those wonderful means—a droll
by-play of wit or humor, a sudden
dash of pathos—by which a master
like Shakspeare throws, as it were in
high, opposed relief, the main action
of the story, Landor makes little use
of.　And hence, though he tells us
that he lived with his personages, and
entered into their sorrows, he never
quite succeeds in creating a complete dramatic illusion.　As in *Sam-
son Agonistes*, the softer human

5

touches, which should finish the picture, are wanting ; and we feel that the poet has not attained the end of his art,—the striking of a perfect mean between the sharply defined individual and the vague type, between the real and the ideal. But perhaps an even stronger reason why the human element is not effective lies in the absence of a well-sustained plot. As Landor conceded, the play is really a series of dramatic dialogues, several of the scenes even interrupting, instead of furthering, the progress of the drama. Furthermore, on the technical side of the dramatist's art, the studied climaxes, the incidental explanations, the efforts to arouse a sense of mystery, of surprise, or of anticipation,—all these are more or less disregarded.

But after all abatements have been made, it is still true that, in Count Julian, Landor had formed a new

and magnificent conception, a conception partaking less of the subtle
complexity of the modern drama,
and more of the simple sublimity of
the antique tragedians,— and one
which he sustained with marvellous
power. De Quincey's words are not
far above the mark when he says:
" Mr. Landor, who always rises with
his subject and dilates like Satan into
Teneriffe or Atlas, when he sees before him an antagonist worthy of his
powers, is probably the one man in
Europe that has adequately conceived the situation, the stern self-
dependency, and the monumental
misery of Count Julian. That sublimity of penitential grief, which
cannot accept consolation from man,
cannot hear external reproach, cannot condescend to notice insult,
cannot so much as *see* the curiosity
of bystanders; that awful careless-
ness of all but the troubled deeps

within his own heart, and of God's spirit brooding upon their surface and searching their abysses, never was so majestically described." Moreover, there are, as we have intimated, superb passages which show their full splendor only when detached and read by themselves. Take the first scene of the fourth act, or better, take the description of Count Julian of which De Quincey was thinking when he wrote the lines quoted above:

" Not victory that o'ershadows him sees
  he ;
 No airy and light passion stirs abroad,
 To ruffle or to soothe him ; all are
  quelled,
 Beneath a mightier, sterner stress of
  mind :
 Wakeful he sits, and lonely, and unmoved,
 Beyond the arrows, views, or shouts
  of men ;

As oftentimes an eagle, ere the sun
Throws o'er the varying earth his
    early ray,
Stands solitary, stands immovable
Upon some highest cliff, and rolls his
    eye,
Clear, constant, unobservant, una-
    based,
In the cold light above the dews of
    morn."

This surely has Miltonic majesty,
and yet the movement, as De Quincey acutely suggested, would have
been amplified and deepened if Landor had placed the line—" Beyond
the arrows, views, or shouts of men "
after what are now the closing words
of the figure, thus making it refer
directly and more appropriately to
the eagle, and at the same time
giving an added depth and impres-
siveness to the close. Landor here,
as in several other places, just comes
short of " the solemn planetary

wheelings " which characterize the sustained and involved harmonies of Milton's blank verse.

In order to reach some final decisions with regard to Landor as a dramatist, one is tempted to contrast him with the greatest of Italian writers of tragedy, Vittorio Alfieri, whom he himself always desired to resemble. In temperament the two men had points in common. Both were possessed of inflammable natures, were on the alert to take offence, and thunderous in their anger. Both had the qualities of the school-boy — quick passions, irrational prejudices, and a somewhat immature enthusiasm for liberators and abhorrence of kings and tyrants —terms which to them were synonymous. There are even superficial likenesses. Both were of good family ; both lived long in voluntary exile ; both detested the French

nation. And as dramatists, the two
had nearly the same ideal, though
they realized it somewhat differ-
ently. Abominating the romanticism which mixes figures and strains
meanings in the vain effort to allego-
rize—which mystifies but does not
enlighten,—they, on the contrary,
aimed to express in clear and vigorous words those universal emotions
which agitate the soul. Their characters, therefore, are not highly
complex organisms, like Hamlet or
Faust, but are rather heroic representations of one or two over-mas-
tering passions. They come upon
the stage, say distinctly what they
feel—in bold, even bald, terms, in
the case of Alfieri, or in chaste and
limpid imagery, in the case of Landor,—and then they vanish. The
complicated development of character, which the novelists, especially,
have delighted to watch, which a

George Eliot has portrayed so wonderfully in Tito Melema, is not
within the range of these students
of the antique. In Alfieri's plays,
in particular, there are no subtle
changes of purpose, no clash of conflicting interests, nothing to retard
the steady, inevitable, on-moving of
the plot. As Mr. Howells has remarked of Alfieri's best tragedy:
" When you read *Orestes*, you find
yourself attendant upon an imma-
nent calamity, which nothing can
avert or delay. In a solitude like
that of dreams, those hapless phan-
tasms, dark types of remorse, of
cruel ambition, of inexorable re-
venge, move swiftly to the fatal end.
They do not grow or develop on
the imagination ; their character is
stamped at once, and they have but
to act it out." This is classicism.
And .it is the ideal of Alfieri and
Landor. From the aspect of form

its effects are finer than any that
romanticism can command. There
is a purity of outline, an incision of
idea, which may not tally with the
exuberance of nature, but which has,
nevertheless, the invaluable charm of
distinctness and finish. Such art
may be selective, and at the same
time natural. Yet, as we have
already noticed, this sculptural
method tends to disregard those
picturesque backgrounds and beautiful contrasts and definite local references which are the life of the
drama. It tends to become as clearly
outlined as a marble statue, and as
cold. But what must inevitably
limit Landor's influence as a dramatist is a defect which he had, but
which Alfieri, fortunately for his
fame, had not. Landor was not
successful in attaining the ideal of
the best Greek art. He did not duly
subordinate the parts to the whole.

His plan is ineffective and inadequately sustained. We are fascinated by exquisite passages, but it is difficult to get a general impression of the whole play. The separate parts do not bind our interest to the development of some central idea. And although we may not demand of a dramatist an exciting plot, we at least demand that he shall stimulate our imagination by suggesting a definite goal, and shall all the while be gradually leading us toward it. Notwithstanding his magnificent conception of Count Julian, this Landor failed to do, and consequently Robert Browning was right in dedicating his *Luria* and *The Soul's Tragedy* to Landor, as being " a great dramatic poet," rather than a great dramatist.

A great dramatist Landor never became, although he composed at least five other tragedies and a comedy. One of the former he seems to have written in 1811 ; but upon learning that Longmans refused to publish *Count Julian*, either at their own, or even at his expense, Landor wrote in great chagrin and exasperation to Southey : " On receiving the last letter of Mr. Longman I committed to the flames my tragedy of *Ferranti and Giulio*, with which I intended to surprise you, and am resolved that never verse of mine shall be hereafter committed to anything else." This storm of indignation, as usual, blew over rapidly ; and *Count Julian* was soon published by Murray, though only a few fragments of the other tragedy had been saved. With the exception of the *Charitable Dowager*, a prose comedy, which Landor was probably wise in not printing, he produced no other complete drama for years. *Count Julian* and the other two plays mentioned above were written at Landor's wild, beautiful residence, Llanthony Abbey, in Wales. Subsequently, on account of hostilities and financial difficulty with tenants and neighbors, Landor had been forced to take up his abode on the continent—first at Tours, then at Como, Pisa, and at last at Florence. He had finally, through the generous advances of Mr. Ablett, a Welsh friend, been able, much to his delight, to purchase the Villa Gherardescha, an exquisite place situated picturesquely on the road which ascends from Florence to Fiesole. And it was while at Florence or at the Villa Gherardescha that Landor accomplished his best work, the wonderful prose embodied in the *Imaginary Conversations*, the *Examination of Shakspeare*, the *Pentameron* and the *Pericles and Aspasia*. Not, however, until he had bid farewell to his beautiful Italian

home, and had taken up his lonely
residence at Bath, did he again try
his hand at tragedy. Here, about
thirty years after the composition of
Count Julian he wrote his dramatic
trilogy, *Andrea of Hungary*, *Giovanna of Naples*, and *Fra Rupert*, and
also his *Siege of Ancona*. Being
laid up with a sprained ankle, he conceived and executed the first of these
dramas in thirteen days, the second
and third were not long in following.
Giovanna of Naples, the Italian
Mary Stuart, who by her tragic surroundings and fascinating personality
had excited Landor's chivalrous susceptibilities, is the subject of the trilogy. And it is needless to say that she
and her several female companions
are portrayed with that subtle insight
into all that is gracious and devoted
in woman's nature, for which Landor
has been so justly praised. The men
are not as successfully handled; yet

the conception of Andrea of Hungary, the young husband of Giovanna, bears the mark of a true artist's workmanship.   Andrea shows, what is rare in Landor's actors, a real development of character.   Brought up under the guardianship of a designing monk, Fra Rupert, he has been purposely allowed to remain in idleness and ignorance, like Shakspeare's Orlando, but his chivalrous soul, under the kind care and compassion of Giovanna, is made to realize itself, by becoming attuned to the chords of love and gratitude.

In general, these plays—including the *Siege of Ancona*, which in manner most resembles *Count Julian*, being pitched in a similarly heroic strain—possess essentially the same merits and defects as Landor's earlier dramatic works.   On the one hand, there is not that effective interaction of characters and motives which,

when regarded from the central idea
of the play, constitutes a definite, co-
herent plot. On the other hand, it is
possible to detach incidents, which,
supposing ourselves acquainted with
the merest outline of the story, may
be viewed as independent imaginary
conversations, and as such are full of
power. Thus, for example, the scene
in the *Siege of Ancona*, wherein the
gentle Lady Malaspina, pressing her
infant to her bosom, laments the
horrors of the famine, is deeply, nobly
pathetic. She whispers to her babe :

" My little one !
God will feed *thee !* Be sleep thy nour-
isher
Until his mercies strengthen me
afresh !"

And when the soldier, with whom she
was conversing, has hurried away to
defend the Balista Gate, she looks
down at the burden in her arms, and
says :

"And still thou sleepest, my sweet babe !
    Is death
Like sleep ? Ah, who then would fear
    to die ?
How beautiful is all serenity ! "

Two priests, passing by, wonder
whether the child over which the
woman leans is dead.   The one
thinks not, because she weeps not
over it ; the other rejoins :

                    " For *that*
    I think it dead.   It then could pierce
        no more
    Her tender heart with its sad sobs and
        cries."

Only a few moments has this "tender heart" to grieve. The Lady Malaspina, unable to resist the fatal inroads
of hunger, lies dead ; and the babe
still peacefully sleeps on her bosom.
    In the same general style as these
separate scenes from Landor's so-

called dramas are the innumerable
short dramatic dialogues, which he
was in the habit of constructing in
verse, as well as in prose, throughout
his life. These animated conversations in metrical form are not essentially different from his prose dialogues of action. The latter are as
likely to be beautifully idealized as
the former ; and the only distinction
between the two classes, is the com-
paratively superficial one of poetic
instead of prose expression. It is
therefore as well to reserve the consideration of Landor's proficiency in
this kind of work, until we come to
notice his *Imaginary Conversations.*
Nevertheless, there are one or two of
these poetic dialogues which for their
haunting beauty may not be put by.
One of these is based upon an imaginary encounter of Menelaus with
Helen, after the fall of Troy. Another, which Landor afterwards em-

7

bodied in the *Pericles and Aspasia* relates to the meeting of Agamemnon and Iphigeneia among the Shades. Of this latter, Landor wrote:

" From eve to morn, from morn to part-
　　　ing night,
　　Father and daughter stood before my
　　　sight.
　　I felt the looks they gave, the words
　　　they said,
　　And reconducted each serener shade.
　　Ever shall these to me be well spent
　　　days,
　　Sweet fell the tears upon them, sweet
　　　the praise ;
　　Far from the footstool of the tragic
　　　throne,
　　I am tragedian in this scene alone."

The dramatic conception of this meeting inheres in the peculiar rela-tions which subsist between father and daughter. Iphigeneia had been sacrificed by Agamemnon on the

outward journey to Troy, in order to
propitiate the gods; and Agamemnon has just been murdered by his
adulterous wife, Clytemnestra. Of
this foul deed, Iphigeneia is profoundly ignorant, and the interest of
the daughter in inquiring about the
living, and especially about her
mother, and at the same time the
unexplained grief and anger of Agamemnon, constitute the dramatic
motive—a potent one. The natural criticism, however, to be passed
upon the scene is, that, while Agamemnon seems gradually to be pre-
paring his daughter for the revelation
of his tragic death, he never really
does tell her. Expectation is excited by his exquisitely managed replies; but no climax is reached. In
reading this dialogue the acute criticism of Chateaubriand with regard
to the pathetic in poetry comes to
our mind as especially applicable.

The condition of father and daughter is truly pathetic; and yet, if our tears are excited, it is "by the beauty of the poetry"—by our admiration rather than by our sorrow. Who can resist the beauty of these lines, especially the Pindaric grandeur of the central ones on Poseidon:

"Father! we must not let you here
      condemn;
  Not, were the day less joyful: recollect
  We have no wicked here; no king to
      judge.
  Poseidon, we have heard, with bitter
      rage
  Lashes his foaming steeds against the
      skies,
  And, laughing with loud yell at
      wingèd fire,
  Innoxious to his fields and palaces,
  Affrights the eagle from the sceptred
      hand;
  While Pluto, gentlest brother of the
      three,

And happiest in obedience, views
    sedate
His tranquil realm, nor envies theirs
    above."

Not only in his dramatic pieces
and in his epic has Landor shown
himself to be a modest master
of the grand in poetry. Two noble
odes, one to Regeneration, the other
to Corinth, at least in places, rise to
the high-water mark of his poetic
attainment. The first half of the
one on Regeneration, which cele-
brates the awakening to liberty of
Italy and Greece in the year 1819, is
thrilling in its enthusiasm. It begins
with the magnificent lines :

"We are what suns, and winds, and
    waters make us ;
  The mountains are our sponsors, and
    the rills
  Fashion and win their nursling with
    their smiles."

Certainly no evolutionary philosopher has ever more grandly
proclaimed the influence of environment! A few lines farther on,
Landor laments the compromising
attitude which England has taken
toward the cause of freedom.

"Oh thou degenerate Albion! with
    what shame
  Do I survey thee, pushing forth the
    sponge
  At thy spear's length, in mocking at
    the thirst
  Of holy Freedom in his agony."

These and others that we might
quote are fine lines; yet it must be
confessed that in this ode, as in
several other lofty poems, Landor is
apt to get involved in the meshes of
a classical reference, and to break
the thread of passion and poetry in
explicating his figure.

Besides all these poetic productions in the grand style, or in a style bordering upon the grand, Landor ran up and down the gamut of the lighter themes of verse. Every passing phase of his experience, from the invitation of a friend to dinner, or the celebration of a loved one's charms, to the separation from his family, or the death of a companion, offers its appropriate dash of color to the picture of his life. Thus his transient moods are wrested from the obliterating stream of consciousness, and preserved in exquisite *eidyllia*, "carvings, as it were, on ivory or on gems." Many of these are erotic, as, for example, those in eulogy of Ianthe, a lady whose real name was Sophia Jane Swift, and whose person and character Landor all his life continued to hold in honorable admiration. What could be nearer to the manner of Catullus, and at the same time happier, than the following tribute to this lady's sunny disposition :

" Your pleasures spring like daisies in
　　the grass,
　Cut down and up again as blithe as
　　ever ;
　From you, Ianthe, little troubles pass,
　　Like little ripples in a sunny river."

Others of these short poems are
invocations or reminiscences of old
familiar objects, with little incidents
now and then interwoven, and a col-
loquial turn given to the swiftly
moving iambics. This work partakes
of the style of Horace. It is Epicurean in implication, yet at the same
time healthy and clean. There is a
naïveté in the quick, picturesque
strokes which is almost irresistible.
Again, Landor writes addresses to
his contemporaries, in the way of
commendation or elegy. There
are odes to Wordsworth and to

Southey. In a poem to the latter
occurs this superb stanza :

" Alas ! that snows are shed
　　Upon thy laurelled head,
Hurtled by many cares and many
　　　　wrongs !
　　Malignity lets none
　　Approach the Delphic throne ;
A hundred lane-fed curs bark down
　　　　Fame's hundred tongues.
But this is in the night when men are slow
To raise their eyes, when high and low,
The scarlet and the colorless, are one :
　　Soon Sleep unbars his noiseless
　　　　prison,
　　And active minds again are risen ;
Where are the curs ? dream-bound and
　　　　whimpering in the sun."

In this ode, however, Landor has
spoiled his climax by not recognizing
that nature in its pristine excellence
should be chosen as imagery rather
than the machinery of literary allu-

sion. Of the elegiac pieces, probably the most perfect is the one written to Mary Lamb on the death of her brother. The rhyme and rhythm of the stanzas accord completely with the sentiment; and the closing lines show Landor's classic mode of expression, his clear uninvolved manner :

"Behold him ! from the region of the
    blest,
  He speaks : he bids thee rest."

Lines like these suggest those beautiful funerary vases, whereon the Greeks were wont to figure the mourners of the departed, standing in simple, touching attitudes, with wreathes in their hands.

It is, however, in the idyl, the last form of poetry attempted by Landor, that we discover his most distinctive poetic contribution. In epic and drama, and even in the occa-

sional pieces, Landor has been out-
stripped by poets of deeper passion
or reflection ; but in his best idyllic
work he has few, if any, superiors.
Tennyson and André Chénier come
to our mind as possible competitors.
Yet the latter had not Landor's
classic restraint and absolute freedom from romanticism ; and the former, in his wonderfully beautiful
Idyls of the King, illustrates what
the French critic calls *simplesse*
rather than real simplicity.

A number of these idyls had origi-
nally appeared in Landor's *Idyllia He-
roica*, in Latin, he having continued
for years to hide away from popular
appreciation interesting prose and
verse by reason of his scholarly, and
at the same time schoolboyish, preference for the language of ancient
Rome over his native tongue. But
at last, at the request of Lady Blessington, Landor agreed to translate

these pieces into English. And as the outcome we have his *Hellenics*. Of all his poetic achievements, these best exhibit what is usually treated as the characteristic note of Greek art—the note of objectivity. Philosophically speaking, this epithet, when applied to an artist, conveys the idea that he has succeeded in great measure in detaching his own subjective interpretation of an object from his observation and portrayal of it ; that he has seen and represented the thing as it is, without trying to suggest any double meaning, any idea of which the corresponding thing is, in Platonic phase, an adumbration. The liquid clearness which results from this objective treatment is the distinctive mark of classicism. And it is in the *Hellenics* that Landor expresses this quality pre-eminently. At the same time it must not be inferred, con-

cerning this kind of art, that the
artist seeks purposely to eliminate
himself and his ideals from the objects of his imagination. It the
rather arises from an inability or dis-
inclination on the part of the poet
to distinguish between nature and
spirit. As a consequence, he does
not swathe the body of sensuous
images, floating on the verge of his
imagination, in the bands of some
preconceived order of intellectual-
ized forms. His soul is a trans-
parent mirror reflecting a series of
refined sensations. And he is so
keenly alive to them, that he is
ready to believe the very rocks are
alive too, and share in the universal
joys of existence. Hence Mr. Forster
is quite right in saying, that Landor
reproduces " the time of light, clear,
definite sensation ; when, to every
man, the shapes of nature were but
the reflection of his own ; when

marvels were not explained but believed, and the supernatural was not higher than the natural, or indeed other than a different development of the attributes and powers of nature."

Among the many fine mythologic themes which compose the *Hellenics*, the finest, the most delightfully objective, is the *Hamadryad*, a poem written in Landor's seventieth year. This idyl perused on a fine day in summer, in some leafy mountain nook, might almost lead the reader, his senses being attuned to the gentle pulsations of its verse, to fancy that he saw, seated there

"Upon the moss below, with her two
    palms
  Pressing it on each side, a maid in
    form,"—

a veritable Hamadryad. And if his mind's eye did not, in the course of his reading, bring out a series of the

most fascinating little pictures, paint-
ed in strokes fascinatingly clear and
delicate, this reader must forsooth be
of dull wits, a dry literalist, dreamless
and imaginationless. Indeed, this
poem of Landor's mature old age is
above analysis. Each image is struck
off with an idealized realism and a
winning yet incisive grace, which
make common adjectives seem nig-
gardly. There are little touches of
characterization, little gnomic expressions on the part of the speakers,
which could not be bettered. What
could be more naïvely feminine than
this :

" Rhoicos went daily ; but the nymph
  as oft,
 Invisible. To play at love, she knew,
 Stopping its breathings when it
  breathes most soft,
 Is sweeter than to play on any pipe.
 She played on his ; she fed upon his
  sighs ;

They pleased her when they gently
    waved her hair,
Cooling the pulses of her purple veins,
And when her absence brought them
    out, they pleased."

Even these few lines, however, give one an idea of the condensation of Landor's style. He is so sparing of words that it is not always easy to tell what his possessive pronouns modify. He is not without faults also in his management of blank verse : instead of keeping his lines relatively entities, he often ends them with a preposition or adjective, either of which is carelessly related to a noun in the succeeding line. Notwithstanding this, many of the *Hellenics* are typical examples of that form of poetry which is of the senses, and is yet pure, clean, and beautiful.

Fitly to close our review of the idyllic poems, and of Landor's poetry in general, we shall quote a few

lines from the *Fiesolan Idyl,* which
will bring before us our author himself, giving us a glimpse of the gen-
tler side of his nature—the side which,
in contrasting it with Landor's vehement outbursts of temper, Leigh
Hunt likened to such a contradiction
in nature as the blossoming of lilies
from a stormy mountain pine. The
close of this poem is open to quotation for its delicate, psychological
perception ; but it is the central
lines, which tell of Landor's love of
flowers, that we especially desire to
transcribe.

" And 't is and ever was my wish and way
    To let all flowers live freely, and all die
    (Whene'er their genius bids their souls
            depart)
    Among their kindred in their native
            place.
    I never pluck the rose ; the violet's head
    Hath shaken with my breath upon its
            bank

8

And not reproached me; the ever
    sacred cup
Of the pure lily hath, between my
    hands,
Felt safe, unsoiled, nor lost one grain of
    gold."

And now with these lines still before us as fair specimens of what Landor could do in the way of verse, we come to ask ourselves, What in general are the elements of power in his poetry? He himself has given a touchstone by which to test his own performance. "What is there in poetry," he makes Boccaccio say, "unless there be moderation and composure? are they not better than the hot, uncontrollable harlotry of a flaunting, dishevelled enthusiasm? Whoever has the power of creating, has likewise the inferior power of keeping his creations in order. The best poets are the most impressive, because their steps are regular; for without regularity there is neither strength nor state." And again, he puts in the mouth of Aspasia the following: "For any high or any wide operation, a poet must be endued, not with passion indeed, but with the power and mastery over it." Now it is acknowledged that Landor's effort after moderation and composure, and the regularity which should result from them, has its fruition in his poetry. He was able to strike off ideas in a singularly vivid, imaginative way, without burdening them with accessory touches, which would obscure their meaning. Doubtless he has also the power and mastery over passion—when the passion is there! but his very fault consists in a lack of that tense enthusiasm and sweeping passion, which are the attributes of great poets. His ideal was more like that of Wordsworth, "emotion remembered in tranquillity "; but then he was not endowed with the the deeply reflective perception which constitutes the glory of Wordsworth. Landor has too little of the transcendentalist about him, too little of the insight that penetrates below the show of things, to possess the power of entering into the inner life of nature and thought. This very fact must forever exclude him from a place among the poets of the front rank. He may have had a modest share of what Matthew Arnold calls " natural magic "; but, barring the really sublime conception of Count Julian, he was practically devoid of " moral profundity." Hence his position and influence as a poet, like that of the æsthetic school of Mr. Swinburne and his compeers— who in a sense recognize themselves as Landor's disciples,—must always remain circumscribed. As Heinrich Heine once said : " Deeds are the off-

spring of words ; but Goethe's pretty
words are childless. That is the
curse upon what has originated in
mere art." And that is the curse
which falls upon much of Landor's
poetry.

III.

LANDOR'S PROSE WRITINGS.

III.

FALLING in with the universal impulse of our day, the tendency to trace derivations, we would find it interesting, were it possible, to study the development of Landor's prose. Certainly a style of such singular excellence could not have been reached without many tentative efforts. Indeed Forster has preserved to us in his *Biography* a letter of Landor's to Dr. Parr which shows the stilted manner of eighteenth-century " epistolary correspondence," and which is of course in marked contrast to the sanity and naturalness which Landor attained in his published prose.

The letter begins: "I am rejoiced to find that you have not forgotten me, and I raise myself up from the bosom of indifference to the voice and the blandishments of praise." We look in vain for such bombast in Landor's later writing, though all through his life we find him inclined to slip into a mode of expression which is declamatory and somewhat Johnsonese. An actual descent into the false sublime, however, is restricted to the political dialogues and pamphlets, which he ever and anon felt constrained to cast upon the troubled waters of civil contention. These, so far as we are acquainted with them, are worthy of his prejudices rather than his powers. Yet it should be said that one often runs across sentences, in the midst of diatribes against priests and kings, which for rhetorical splendor are unsurpassed and unsurpassable. And it must also be said that Landor's opposition to war, and enthusiasm for freedom justly challenge our admiration and adherence—at least in their general conception, if not in their Landorian applications.

Omitting the consideration of Landor's political writings, and of his pleas for spelling-reform, which were generally unheeded; of his occasional essays in criticism, which, with the exception of three refined textual studies of Theocritus, Catullus, and Petrarch, have not come down to us ; and of his Latin works, which we would scarcely have the temerity to criticise, even were they perfectly preserved,—we have remaining four great monuments in prose, the *Imaginary Conversations*, the *Citation and Examination of William Shakspeare*, the *Pentameron*, and the *Pericles and Aspasia.*

It was after Landor had gotten

comfortably established in Italy that he wrote, between the years 1821 and 1829, the major part of the first of these works. His inclination had always been toward this mode of expression. Twenty years before, he had offered to the *Morning Chronicle*, the organ of the Whigs, among whom he then counted himself an unbiassed exponent, a dialogue between Burke and Grenville. This had not been accepted, and he does not appear to have made many more attempts at this kind of writing until after he had taken up his abode in Florence in the fall of 1821. Landor's concrete way of looking at things, his ready enthusiasm for persons embodying certain sentiments and ideas, rather than for the abstract, logical presentation of these ideas and sentiments, made the dialogue his natural literary element. He was almost as much of a hero-worshipper as Carlyle. The

Hegelian conception of a collective, or rather of an organic, humanity advancing from age to age, at one time with halting step, at another with assurance and courage, toward the more perfect realization of the divine idea, would have seemed to him but a mystical ideal for one to set before all thoughtful men as the goal toward which they must strive, yea, even agonize. It would indeed have been well if the following magnificent words written by Mazzini had been pondered by these intense individualists, Carlyle and Landor: "There is something greater, more divinely mysterious, than all the great men—and that is the human race which includes them, the thought of God which stirs within them, and which the whole human race collectively can alone accomplish. Disown not, then, the common mother for the sake of certain of her children, however privileged they may be; for at the same time that you disown her, you will lose the true comprehension of these rare men whom you admire. . . . The inspiration of genius belongs one half to heaven, the other to the crowd of common mortals from whose life it springs." Such a conception of the solidarity and interconnection of the race, coupled with the idea of a God in and at the same time above humanity, might well arouse our aspirations and our efforts. And it is far removed from the Comtean view which, instead of recognizing God as working in humanity and yet above it, identifies, by a debasing anthropomorphism, the idea of Deity with the notion of collective man, and thus gives the sanction of divinity to mere numbers; whereas it is indeed difficult to see how, if individual man be not God-born, hu-

manity, or collective man, can possess
this attribute. The whole cannot be
different from its parts; and if the
individual be without God in the
world, even so must be the race.
These high ideas, however, were not
within Landor's range of thought.
An admiration for individual traits
was the mainspring in his theory of
life. He quotes enthusiastically, in
one of his letters, the following lines
from the *Life of Blanco White*, which
adequately sum up his own philosophy: " The moral world presents
upon the whole a most hideous and
distorted appearance. But it hap-
pens here, as in some pictures.
Looked at with the naked eye, they
are a perfect mass of confusion ;
but the moment you look through
a lens constructed to unite the
scattered lines in a proper focus,
they show a regularity, and even
beauty. My favorite lens is a vir-

tuous man ; it brings into harmony the discordant parts of the moral world."

For the representation, in imaginary conversations, of the virtuous and the wise of the past, Landor was, moreover, especially fitted by his general intellectual make-up. Inconsecutiveness, which in other forms of prose would be counted a fault, is unobjectionable in the dialogue, if kept within the large, embracing unity of a central thought. And the opportunity, by virtue of the freedom and informality of conversation, to give vent to extravagant ideas peculiar to the author is likewise made possible. This is a concession important to a writer possessed of Landor's impetuous individuality. So that, when speaking in the person of another, he could in reality express his own idiosyncrasies more freely than if he had chosen to write *in propria persona* through the medium of essay or treatise.

Landor availed himself of this license even to the choice of subjects, taking his characters indiscriminately from many nationalities and many ages ; so that it is not easy to establish a classification of the dialogues, with the divisions complete and mutually exclusive. The best arrangement that has been suggested is by Mr. Colvin, who distinguishes between the dramatic and the non-dramatic conversations. This is certainly a philosophic demarcation, and one which can be applied with some degree of exactitude. We would, however, prefer to employ the positive terms, reflective and dramatic, in discriminating between the two classes.

The dialogues of reflection are usually long, not always easy to read through without weariness, yet

9

abound in original and penetrating aphorisms couched in strikingly beautiful imagery. There are, however, two vital defects in the reflective class, which, if they do not lower the high value of selections from the conversations, do certainly modify our appreciation of them as wholes. The first of these defects may be seen by contrasting Landor with Plato. Emerson truly says: " Plato turns incessantly the obverse and the reverse of the medal of Jove." By this he primarily meant that Plato had the abstract speculative genius of the Oriental coupled with the love of the accomplished fact which characterizes our Western mind ; but he also meant to infer that in the dialogues Plato saw both sides of a question, so that his speakers could always give the *cons* as well as the *pros*. This versatility Landor's characters do not possess. Our author

is not proficient in the play of re-
partee, which really constitutes the
life of the dialogue. Timotheus or
Calvin are the mere targets at which
Lucian or Melancthon level their
controversial guns. And the poor
targets become thoroughly riddled
before the conversations are over.
The sense of friction, of clash, which
should sustain our flagging interest,
is conspicuously absent. And, consequently, our wits are not aroused to
a fascinated play of thought, and
our attention begins to wane.

The other defect, which is fully as
serious, arises from the lack of organic unity in the several conversations. We do not, of course, mean
that Landor should have analytically
plotted out a dialogue, as one would
divide a treatise, making the various
parts depend explicitly and obviously
upon some central conception. Such
a design would have stopped the flow

of imagination, and have rendered
the speeches stilted and unreal. But
we do mean that Landor should
himself have known whither he was
leading us, and that the meandering
paths of thought should have at last
opened out upon some central pros-
pect, whence we might look down
and discover the way we had come.
Landor should have recognized that
a vast body of aphorisms and fine
thoughts, and also, it must be acknowledged, of tedious disquisitions,
must collapse into an incoherent
mass if they be not sustained by the
skeleton of an underlying idea. That
he did not recognize this fact is seen
from his own figurative account of
his mode of composing the dialogues.
" I confess to you," he says, " that a
few detached thoughts and images
have always been the beginnings of
my works.   Narrow slips have risen
up, more or fewer, above the sur-

face. These gradually became larger and more consolidated; freshness and verdure first covered one part, then another; then plants of firmer and higher growth, however scantily, took their places, then extended their roots and branches; and among them, and around about them, in a little while you yourself, and as many more as I desired, found places for study and recreation." Thus, instead of constructing each of these conversations after the model of a tree, Landor has chosen to make each represent a whole tangled forest of oaks and underbrush. A true dialogue, like a true poem, should contain within itself, not openly, but in implication, a thoroughly thought-out plan. This Landor failed to see, and hence fell short of the ideal requirements.

But after we have made all our admissions, it must still be allowed that these conversations contain—as Landor himself declared, when his exasperation was excited by difficulties in publishing them—" as forcible writing as exists on earth." Not only are they forcible ; many of them are pervaded by a spirit of beauty that is rarely attained. Take the dialogue between Epicurus and his two lovely pupils, Leontion and Ternissa. The Epicureanism, which would environ us amid delightful sights and sounds and would thus gently withdraw our souls away from the din of the crowd into the peace of self-culture and self-satisfaction, was never more alluringly set forth. " Oh, sweet sea-air ! how bland art thou, and refreshing ! breathe upon Leontion ! breathe upon Ternissa ! bring them health and spirits and serenity, many springs and many summers, and when the vine-leaves have reddened and rustle under their feet. These, my beloved girls, are the children of Eternity. They played around Theseus and the beauteous Amazon; they gave to Pallas the bloom of Venus, and to Venus the animation of Pallas. Is it not better to enjoy by the hour their soft salubrious influence, than to catch by fits the rancid breath of demagogues ; than to swell and move under it without or against our will ; than to acquire the semblance of eloquence by the bitterness of passion, the tone of philosophy by disappointment, or the credit of prudence by distrust ? Can fortune, can industry, can desert itself, bestow on us anything we have not here?"

Again, take the conversation between Vittoria Colonna and Michael Angelo, wherein they discuss the qualities of poetry and the glory of the Greeks. How acute and true are the following aphorisms: " The beautiful in itself is useful by awak-

ening our finer sensibilities, which it
must be our own fault if we do not
carry with us into action."—"Wishes
are by-paths on the declivity to un-
happiness; the weaker terminate in
the sterile sand, the stronger in
the vale of tears."—"Serenity is no
sign of security. A stream is never
so smooth, equable, and silvery, as at
the instant before it becomes a cata-
ract. The children of Niobe fell by
the arrows of Diana under a bright
and cloudless sky."—"Little minds
in high places are the worst impedi-
ments to great. Chestnuts and es-
culent oaks permit the traveller to
pass onward under them; briars and
thorns and unthrifty grass entangle
him." The last two quotations give
the mechanism of Landor's prose—
first the simple statement of an idea,
then a metaphor illustrative of it.

Two of the most suggestive of the
reflective dialogues have already

been mentioned in another connection, those between Lucian and
Timotheus, and Calvin and Melancthon. These illustrate what we have
called Landor's religious positivism.
In the former, the pagan satirist,
who is Landor himself in thin disguise, gets the better of his cousin,
the Christian Timotheus, and in the
course of the argument gives expression to this characteristic remark:
" We are upon earth to learn what
can be learnt upon earth, and not to
speculate on what never can be . . .
Let men learn what benefits men;
above all things, to contract their
wishes, to calm their passions, and,
more especially, to dispel their fears.
Now they are to be dispelled, not by
collecting clouds, but by piercing
and scattering them. In the dark
we may imagine depths and heights
immeasurable, which, if a torch be
carried right before us, we find it

easy to leap across. Much of what we call sublime is only the residue of infancy, and the worst of it." It is curious that Kant is reported to have expressed the same idea as is contained in the last two sentences, in reference to the poetry of Isaiah and Ossian. Both men, as rationalists, were constitutionally unable to realize that the profound synthetic intuitions of the poet are sublime, not because of an obscurity which is incident to human limitations, but by reason of the divine hints, which these intuitions contain, of higher spiritual altitudes and loftier issues than man had before dreamed of.

In the discussion between Calvin and Melancthon, the former is as clay in the hands of his humanitarian opponent. This is surely an unfair representation of the acknowledged logical acumen of the great Genevan theologian. Nevertheless,

Melancthon enunciates several sentiments which it would have been well
if Calvin and some of his theological
successors had thoughtfully heeded.
Thus he says, somewhat after the
manner of Emerson or Matthew Arnold : " What a curse hath metaphor
been to religion ! It is the wedge
that holds asunder the two great
portions of the Christian world. We
hear of nothing so commonly as fire
and sword. And here, indeed, what
was metaphor is converted into sub-
stance and applied to practice."
Again, he says : " I remember no
discussion on religion in which religion was not a sufferer by it, if
mutual forbearance and belief in another's good motives and intentions
are (as I must always think they are)
its proper and necessary appurte-
nances." How identical this sentiment is with the life and thought of
our great American teacher, Emer-

son! And again, near the close of the dialogue, Melancthon makes some searching remarks concerning idolatry, discussing it very much as a Greek philosopher would, and at last uttering this humanitarian principle: "But in regard to idolatry, I see more criminals that are guilty of it than you do. I go below the stone-quarry and the pasture, beyond the graven image and the ox-stall. If we bow before the distant image of good, while there exists within our reach one solitary object of substantial sorrow, which sorrow our efforts can remove, we are guilty (I pronounce it) of idolatry. We prefer the intangible effigy to the living form. Surely we neglect the service of our Maker if we neglect his children." This religion of kindly common-sense is again expounded by William Penn in his dialogue with Lord Peterborough, who represents the aristocrat with ideals out of joint with the actual condition of the aristocracy. Landor is here able to give voice to his oft repeated disgust for a democracy, which must needs be devoid of nobility and distinction. Landor thoroughly concurred in Pascal's saying : "*A mesure qu'on a plus d'esprit on trouve qu'il y a plus d'hommes originaux. Les gens du commun ne trouvent pas de différence entre les hommes.*"

Without taking the space to dilate upon the fine old Roman dignity which permeates the dialogues between Lucullus and Cæsar, and Cicero and his brother, we must select finally, as bringing out an element in Landor's character, the conversations between Chesterfield and Chatham, and Diogenes and Plato, both of these having for their object to exhibit the last-named philosopher in a light decidedly unfavorable to his reputation. As Mr. Colvin has pointed out, Landor had spent weeks in strenuously reading all the Platonic dialogues in the original. This examination must have been somewhat perfunctory; and partly as the result of it, Landor conceived an invincible dislike for what he held to be the "bodiless incomprehensible vagaries" and the falsely ornate style of Plato; therefore he makes this philosopher appear as a ridiculous milksop of a sophist in the presence of his gruff contemporary of the Tub; and even when Plato indulges in a fine figure like this, "The brightest of stars appear the most unsteady and tremulous in their light, not from any quality inherent in themselves, but from the vapors that float below, and from the imperfection of vision in the surveyor," Diogenes roughly retorts, " Draw thy robe around thee; let the folds fall gracefully, and look majestic. That sentence is an admirable one; but not for me. I want sense, not stars." Diogenes here gives, more or less truly, Landor's real thought concerning Plato, and concerning even the faintest tincture of so-called mysticism. This attitude toward the Greek thinker shows, characteristically, an obvious limitation in Landor's intelligence. His mind clung only too tenaciously to the tangible; and speculative insight, the power of drawing the universal out of its investiture in particulars, he therefore undervalued, designating its products by some such opprobrious epithets as "bodiless incomprehensible vagaries." In this, Landor is another example of the tendency to depreciate that particular faculty which one does not happen to possess.

While the dialogues of reflection

are thus somewhat too heavily freighted with Landor's idiosyncrasies, and are likewise open to the two general defects of being one-sided in opinion and deficient in organic unity, the dialogues of action are amenable to none of these objections, but are scenes transcribed from the drama of history with as masterful a hand as any within the range of classical literature. These dialogues are especially and justly noted for their delicate insight into womanhood. In a letter to Southey Landor makes us aware of the source of this power. "I delight," he says, "in the minute variations and almost imperceptible shades of the female character, and confess that my reveries, from my most early youth, were almost entirely on what this one or that one would have said or done in this or that situation. Their countenances, their movements, their forms, the colors of their dresses, were before my eyes." In the concrete realization of these reveries in such personages as Anne Boleyn, Lady Lisle, Jeanne D'Arc, Vipsania, and Godiva, the original glow of his imagination shines with undiminished brightness and beauty.

Thus, the unfortunates, Vipsania and Anne Boleyn, in their womanly patience and innocency stand in touching contrast to their husbands, the weak-willed Tiberius and the brutal Henry. Another attractive female character is Rhodope, who tells to her fellow-slave, Æsop, the story of a famine during which her father was forced to sell her into slavery. Parts of this dialogue are in Landor's best style. Yet it is always true of him that in narratives introduced in the midst of the conversation he is apt to grow tedious and to violate probability. Thus,

10

Rhodope, though only five years of age when the famine occurred, and now only fourteen, recalls the details connected with it as if she had been a grown woman. Her memory of the incidents is more than precocious, it is prematurely old ; and she reminds us of one of those diminutive adults that are represented by early sculptors in default of children. Thus a child of five years has the sagacity to know the estimation in which her "father had always been held by his fellow-citizens," and the precocity to pinch his ear, as a playful way of arousing his anger against one of his friends. Nor can we defend this unreality by supposing that Rhodope's present developed personality colors the memory of her past experience, since even at the time of her relating the story she is a mere girl of fourteen.

A more successful dialogue, and

one which gives us a glimpse of the
sweetest, purest, and most compas-
sionate of all Landor's women, is that
between the Lady Godiva and her
husband, Earl Leofric. It would be
hard to find in literature a more beautiful and touching conception than
that of the tender-hearted Lady Godiva, pleading with all the enticements
of love and all the power of an angel,
that thus she may prevail upon her
obdurate lord to remit the tax, which
his starving tenants are unable to
pay, even after the utmost self-de-
denial. Thus, when Leofric declares
that the tax must be paid, else solemn
festivals cannot be held, Godiva rejoins: " Is the clamorousness that
succeeds the death of God's dumb
creatures, are crowded halls, are
slaughtered cattle, festivals? are
maddening songs and giddy dances,
and hireling praises from party-col-
ored coats? Can the voice of a

minstrel tell us better things of
ourselves than our own internal one
might tell us? or can his breath
make our breath softer in sleep?
Oh my beloved! let everything be a
joyance to us; it will, if we will.
Sad is the day, and worse must follow, when we hear the blackbird in
the garden and do not throb with
joy. But, Leofric, the high festival
is strown by the servant of God upon
the heart of man. It is gladness, it
is thanksgiving; it is the orphan,
the starveling, pressed to the bosom,
and bidden, as its first command-
ment, to remember its benefactor.
We will hold this festival, the guests
are ready. We may keep it up for
weeks, and months, and years together, and always be the happier
and richer for it. The beverage of
this feast, O Leofric, is sweeter than
bee or flower or vine can give us:
it flows from heaven; and in heaven

will it abundantly be poured out again, to him who pours it out here unsparingly." The angelic spirit with which the lady nerves herself to obey the cruel requirement which her spouse, partly in jest and partly in vexation, had laid upon her, that he might thus induce her to desist from the request, is a fit climax to this most perfect of the conversations.

Dialogues very different from these and from each other, are the ones between Metellus and Marius, and Peter the Great and his son Alexis. Each illustrates a phase of Landor's talent. The former with its stupendous conception of "the civic fire" portrays the insatiable spirit of Roman conquest; the latter, Landor's harsh, rugged manner in his satires. It was impossible for him to condone what is base or cruel, so that his satire resembles Juvenal's or Swift's, more than Horace's or Thackeray's. He aims to be extravagant and crushing rather than mildly derisive, and distorts the facts, not mockingly, but with a profound sense of anger for outraged justice.

As showing another feature of Landor's talent, namely, the way in which he took the bare intimations of history and clothed them by the power of a suggestive, sympathetic imagination, we might instance the dialogue between the Earl of Essex and Edmund Spenser. Probably the only historic material for this finely conceived scene is to be found in the following statement of Ben Jonson, as reported by his literary compeer, Drummond of Hawthornden : " The Irish having rob'd Spenser's goods, and burnt his house and a little child new-born, he and his wife escaped; and after, he died for lake of bread, in King street, and refused 20 pieces sent to him by my Lord of Essex, and said he was sorrie he had no time to spend them." Landor used to say of himself : " I am a horrible. confounder of historical facts ; I have usually one history that I have read, and another that I have invented." The truth of the acknowledgment is seen in this dialogue, whose dramatic motive, as invented by Landor, lies in Essex's ignorance of the reason for the poet's grief, and in the gradual revelation of its cause, and in the exquisite tact and kindness with which the Earl seeks to lighten the grievous burden of his unfortunate friend. Another dialogue even more pathetic, and one, moreover, which rises to the very summit of sublimity, is that between Lady Lisle and Elizabeth Gaunt. The humility and complete self-abnegation shown by these heroic souls are conceived with loving fidelity; and the depth of Christian feeling displayed makes us almost willing to take back the assertion, made in treating of Landor as a man of letters, that the Christian ideal of self-sacrifice was foreign to his nature. In such dialogues as this, one realizes that if Landor did not follow the exact facts of the past, he so transfused and irradiated the spirit of history as to render the notice of his departure from minute accuracy unessential and ill-timed.

The style of these dialogues of action is as interesting a study as their subject-matter. In them, Landor often carries his tendency to condensation of phrase and thought to an extreme. He gives no stage directions, and we have constantly to imagine what the actors are doing, in order that we may catch the thread of their intercourse. Thus, we must picture Godiva, as having dismounted and as kneeling by the side of the road, petitioning Leofric's mercy toward his vassals; when suddenly he exclaims: " Here comes the bishop: we are but one mile from the walls. Why dismountest thou? No bishop can expect it. Godiva! my honor and my rank among men are humbled by this: Earl Godwin will hear of it. Up! up! the bishop hath seen it; he urgeth his horse onward. Dost thou not hear him now upon the solid turf behind thee?" At times, this mode of indirectly incorporating what are really stage directions, into the dialogue, gives us an unpleasant jar; because we feel that one actor is describing to the other what must be already patent to both, and that this is done merely for the sake of making the situation plain to the audience.

Another peculiarity is the maintenance of sober and regularly constructed sentences even in the midst of the highest excitement and passion. This tendency, already noted, leads to a peculiar psychological effect upon the reader. It makes him more directly moved by the attractive management of the situation than by its inherent pathos or sublimity. Our critical appreciation is never held in abeyance. Hence the qualities of Landor's work appeal to us more as artists than simply as men. We always remain conscious of its technical finish. The emotions experienced by the character, while conceived with all fidelity, yet their expression being sober and regular, and not, as in life, harsh and disjointed, the scene is removed a step from the actual, and we are unable to enter spontaneously into the rush of feeling, but must admire while keeping relatively unmoved. These facts explain why Landor, like Edmund Spenser, may be called "a writer's writer."

If this epithet might be applied to the author of the *Imaginary Conversations,*—typical specimens of which, we have tried to select from among the one hundred and forty-seven dialogues,—much more is it applicable to one who wrote the *Citation and Examination of William Shakspeare before the Worshipful Sir Thomas Lucy, Knight, touching Deerstealing.* This amplified conversation Landor composed while at his beautiful Italian home, the Villa Gherardescha, where he lived from 1829 to 1837, and where he also wrote the *Pericles and Aspasia,* and a part of the *Pentameron.* The *Examination,* which is an elaborate essay at humor conveyed in the heavily loaded style of Elizabethan prose, is the least happy of all Landor's longer writings. He himself expressed some doubts as to whether his humor would seem humorous — doubts which were amply sustained by the result. The attempt to retain evanescent flashes of wit within a euphuistic style laden with formalities and circumlocutions is as though one should try to spirit about a bludgeon as if it were a rapier. Wit and humor of this description tend to become ponderous and depressing ; and this is just what Landor's efforts at the facetious actually are. One easily recognizes other defects. The freedom of epithet and of reference, not to say the indecency of an occasional remark, particularly one from Sir Silas, may be characteristic of Elizabethan literature, but fortunately is not of Victorian. Indeed, Landor has reproduced this element with more historic accuracy than he has some others worthier of reproduction. Thus, for example, the verses discovered in the culprit's pocket are much more Landorian than Shakspearian. And Shakspeare himself, in the person of a decidedly pert young man, would hardly lead one to infer the presence of a universal genius.

The grandiloquent knight, who prides himself upon his gentle birth and his knowledge of poetry and theology, and his malicious chaplain, Master Silas Gough, who entertains designs upon Shakspeare's sweetheart, Anne Hathaway, are more happily conceived, in a vein of humor somewhere between mere exaggeration and caricature. And the clever sayings which the former sometimes throws out to his dependants, as well as the weighty words which Shakspeare is made to quote from Dr. Glaston, an Oxford preacher, are well worth digging out and scrutinizing. The entire narrative of the pathetic fate of the young poet, John Wellerby, which Shakspeare is supposed to have heard from Dr. Glaston, is permeated with an ideal beauty, making it by far the finest passage in this disappointing book.

The *Pentameron*, another conversation elaborated into a small volume, is much more successful both in choice of subject and in treatment. It purports to be five interviews, held on five successive days, between Boccaccio, who is ill, and his sympathetic friend, Petrarch, who has come to visit him. The title and idea of the book are of course taken from Boccaccio's *Decameron*, which always appealed to Landor, doubtless above its actual value. Boccaccio's honest and lusty, if sometimes coarse, realism, his hearty grasp upon certain types of character, his power as a story-teller — all aroused Landor's admiration. And moreover, on the very grounds about the villa where Landor lived lay the Valley of Ladies, described in the *Decameron;* and, as Forster says, from Landor's "gate up to the gates of Florence there was hardly a street or farm that the great story-teller had not associated with some witty or affecting narrative." Such scenes were naturally calculated to quicken Landor's imagination, and to intensify his interest in Boccaccio.

It were useless in examining a book as delightful as this, some of whose pages, as Mrs. Browning said, "are too delicious to turn over," to do other than allow it to interpret itself. Its three most striking features, its episodes, allegories, and criticisms, are best seen by quotation, the only difficulty in such a course being, that, amid such fascinating and quotable material, it is impossible to resist the temptation of transcribing one more sentence, and you are thus irresistibly lured on.

Take these scraps of the episode relating to Petrarch's visit to the parish church at Certaldo. "It being now the Lord's Day, Messer Francesco thought it meet that he should rise early in the morning and bestir himself, to hear mass in the parish church at Certaldo. Whereupon he went on tiptoe, if so weighty a man could indeed go in such a fashion, and lifted softly the latch of Ser Giovanni's chamber door, that he might salute him ere he departed, and occasion no wonder at the step he was about to take. . . . He then went into the kitchen, where he found the girl Assunta, and mentioned his resolution. . . . But Ser Francesco, with his natural politeness, would not allow her to equip his palfrey. 'This is not the work for maidens,' said he ; 'return to the house, good girl!' She lingered a moment, then went away ; but, mistrusting the dexterity of Ser Francesco, she stopped and turned back again, and peeped through the half-closed door, and heard sundry sobs and wheezes around about the girth. Ser Francesco's wind ill seconded his intention ; and, although he had thrown the saddle valiantly and stoutly in its station, yet the girths brought him into extremity. She entered again, and dissembling the reason, asked him whether he would not take a small beaker of the sweet white wine before he set out, and offered to girdle the horse while his Reverence bitted and bridled him. Before any answer could be returned, she had begun. And having now satisfactorily executed her undertaking, she felt irresistible delight and glee at being able to do what Ser

Francesco had failed in. He was scarcely more successful in his allotment of the labor—found unlooked-for intricacies and complications in the machinery, wondered that human wit could not simplify it, and declared that the animal never had exhibited such restiveness before. In fact, he had never experienced the same grooming."

Although Landor expressed his own belief when he represented Petrarch as saying: "Allegory had few attractions for me, believing it to be the delight in general of idle, frivolous, inexcursive minds, in whose mansions there is neither hall nor portal to receive the loftier of the passions"; yet for picturesqueness of expression and transparency of sentiment, the allegories, in the form of dreams, which Boccaccio and Petrarch relate to each other, are unsurpassed in the prose literature of imagination. Notice this fine consolatory description of Death in Petrarch's allegory of Sleep, Love, and Death. "At last, before the close of the altercation between Love and Sleep, the third Genius had advanced, and stood before us. I cannot tell how I knew him, but I knew him to be the Genius of Death. Breathless as I was at beholding him, I soon became familiar with his features. First they seemed calm; presently they grew contemplative; and lastly beautiful: those of the Graces themselves are less regular, less harmonious, less composed. Love glanced at him unsteadily, with a countenance in which there was somewhat of anxiety, somewhat of disdain; and cried: 'Go away! go away! nothing that thou touchest, lives!' 'Say rather, child!' replied the advancing form, and advancing grew loftier and statelier,—

' Say rather that nothing of beautiful or of glorious lives its own true life until my wing hath passed over it.' Love pouted, and rumpled and bent down with his forefinger the stiff, short feathers on his arrowhead ; but replied not. Although he frowned worse than ever, and at me, I dreaded him less and less, and scarcely looked toward him."

Of criticisms and of general reflections, most of them upon literary topics, the *Pentameron* has a delightful profusion. " No advice is less necessary to you," Landor says, through the thin disguise of Petrarch, " than the advice to express your meaning as clearly as you can. Where the purpose of glass is to be seen through, we do not want it tinted or wavy." Again, it is really Landor who says : " Enter into the mind and heart of your own creatures ; think of them long, en-

tirely, solely; never of style, never
of self, never of critics, cracked or
sound. Like the miles of an open
country, and of an ignorant popula-
tion, when they are correctly meas-
ured they become smaller. In the
loftiest rooms and richest entabla-
tures are suspended the most spider-
webs; and the quarry out of which
palaces are erected is the nursery of
nettle and bramble." It is to be
regretted that Landor failed to perceive, however, that these spider-
webs, these obscurities, arising from
a lack of consideration for one's audience, are just what rightly frighten
away the majority of the reading
public.

In the direct line of literary criticism, Landor expends his energies
upon Horace, Virgil, and Dante.
When treating of the great Florentine, it were well if he had kept in
mind his own words, which he puts

into the mouth of Petrarch: " Systems of poetry, of philosophy, of government, form and model us to their own proportions." This fact is precisely what Landor overlooks when he comes to examine Dante. He seems to be oblivious of the truth that the great poet, notwithstanding his unique, lofty, and omnipresent personality, was an integral part of his age and its highest expression, and that to appreciate him in any true degree the imagination must travel back to the Middle Ages, to Dante's environment, through the doors of approach found in the history of popes and emperors, of the Italian cities and of scholasticism. Landor, on the contrary, studies Dante as an isolated phenomenon—as we have already had occasion to remark ; and partly for this reason, reaches the very debatable conclusion that in the whole of the *Inferno* the only descriptions at all admirable are the episode of Francesca, so tenderly human as it is, though atmosphered by despair, and that of Ugolino. "Vigorous expressions there are many, but lost in their application to base objects; and isolated thoughts in high relief, but with everything crumbling around them. Proportionately to the extent, there is a scantiness of poetry, if delight be the purpose or indication of it. Intensity shows everywhere the powerful master: and yet intensity is not invitation. A great poet may do everything but repel us. Established laws are pliant before him: nevertheless his office hath both its duties and its limits."

It is impossible to close this converse with Petrarch and Boccaccio without transcribing the following thoughts, which, in their nobility, are not unlike Cicero's meditations upon friendship and old age. Petrarch says: "O Giovanni! the heart that has once been bathed in love's pure fountain, retains the pulse of youth forever. Death can only take away the sorrowful from our affections: the flower expands, the colorless film that enveloped it falls off and perishes." Boccaccio replies: "We may well believe it: and believing it, let us cease to be disquieted for their absence who have but retired into another chamber. We are like those who have overslept the hour: when we rejoin our friends, there is only the more joyance and congratulation. Would we break a precious vase, because it is as capable of containing the bitter as the sweet? No: the very things which touch us the most sensibly are those which we should be the most reluctant to forget. The noble mansion is most distinguished by the

beautiful images it retains of beings
past away; and so is the noble
mind. The damps of autumn sink
into the leaves and prepare them for
the necessity of their fall: and thus
insensibly are we, as years close
around us, detached from our te-
nacity of life by the gentle pressure
of recorded sorrows."

The *Pentameron* was immediately
preceded by the *Pericles and Aspasia*, a work which we have chosen
to treat last, because we regard it as
pre-eminently Landor's masterpiece.
Though writing without books of
reference, and with his usual determination not to put into the mouth
of his speakers any words which history has attributed to them, Landor
was yet able marvellously to repro-
duce the serenely attractive atmosphere of the Periclean age, and to
fill his canvas with a succession
of fair forms and characteristically

Greek, and at the same time Landorian reflections, such as no other modern has ever succeeded in doing. The volume is *sui generis*, and will probably long remain so ; moreover, unlike Landor's other compositions, no excisions could be made in it without weakening the general effect. Of course the antiquary might discover anachronisms and historic inaccuracies ; but then his interference here, as in Shakspeare's plays, is often an impertinence—an insistence upon the letter and a disregard of the spirit.

Moreover, the ideas being cast in the form of letters, between Pericles and his wife and between her and her friends, the objections involved in Landor's conduct of the dialogue are of none effect. It would be unnatural for letters, which presuppose decided intervals of time between their composition, and different moods in the writers, to maintain strict organic unity and sequence among themselves. That the replies are as spontaneous and irregular as in life, introducing any passing impressions or ideas of the correspondent and any incident or conversation in which he happened to take part, constitutes the central charm of this form of writing. The lack of an elaborate plot or plan, which in other compositions would be counted a weakness, is not so here. The result tends rather to produce a satisfying sense of beautiful and chaste reality.

And as giving at least a faint idea of the finish and fascination of these letters, take the closing words of a missive, written by Aspasia to her young girl friend Cleone, descriptive of Alcibiades, then a youth : " He is as beautiful, playful, and uncertain as any half-tamed young tiger, feasted and caressed on the royal carpets of Persepolis; not even Aspasia will ever quite subdue him." Then mark Cleone's reply: "I shall never more be in fear about you, my Aspasia. Frolicsome and giddy as you once appeared to me, at no time of your life could Alcibiades have interested your affections. You will be angry with me when I declare to you that I do not believe you will ever be in love. The renown and genius of Pericles won your imagination: his preference, his fondness, his constancy, hold, and will ever hold, your heart. The very beautiful rarely love at all. Those precious images are placed above the reach of the Passions: Time alone is permitted to efface them; Time, the father of the gods, and even *their* consumer." Note the frank, feminine rejoinder of Aspasia: "Angry! yes, indeed, very angry am I: but let me lay all my anger in the right place. I was often jealous of your beauty, and have told you so a thousand times. Nobody for many years ever called me so beautiful as Cleone ; and when some people did begin to call me so, I could not believe them. Few will allow the first to be first ; but the second and third are universal favorites. We are all insurgents against the despotism of excellence."

Again, take this scrap which introduces three of the greatest names of Greece. Aspasia writes to Cleone : " We were conversing on oratory and orators, when Anaxagoras said, looking at Pericles and smiling, ' They are described by Hesiod in two verses, which he applies to himself and the poets :

Lies very like the truth we tell,
And, when we wish it, truth as well.'

Meton relaxed from his usual seriousness, but had no suspicion of the application, saying, 'Cleverly applied indeed!' Pericles enjoyed the simplicity of Meton and the slyness of Anaxagoras, and said, 'Meton! our friend Anaxagoras is so modest a man, that the least we can do for him is to acknowledge his claims as heir general to Hesiod. See them registered.' I have never observed the temper of Pericles either above or below the enjoyment of a joke; he invites and retaliates, but never begins, lest he should appear to take a liberty. There are proud men of so much delicacy, that it almost conceals their pride, and perfectly excuses it." This last sentiment Landor no doubt felt would apply to himself as well.

As an example of a different order of thought, let us transcribe the parting words of Pericles when on his death-bed: "'Alcibiades! I need not warn you against superstition: it

never was among your weaknesses.
Do not wonder at these amulets:
above all, do not order them to be
removed. The kind old nurses, who
have been faithfully watching over
me day and night, are persuaded
that these will save my life. Superstition is rarely so kind-hearted ;
whenever she is, unable as we are
to reverence, let us at least respect
her. After the good, patient creatures have found, as they must soon,
all their traditional charms unavail-
ing, they will surely grieve enough,
and perhaps from some other motive
than their fallibility in science. In-
flict not, O Alcibiades, a fresh wound
upon their grief, by throwing aside
the tokens of their affection. In
hours like these we are the most
indifferent to opinion, and greatly
the most sensible to kindness.' The
statesman, the orator, the conqueror,
the protector, had died away ; the

philosopher, the humane man, yet was living . . . alas! few moments more."

Some of Landor's most characteristic utterances on the great subjects of human thought are to be found among these letters. Thus, viewing history, not from the modern standpoint of Vico and his successors, who perceive within historic facts the unity of a progressively unfolding idea, but from the individualistic standpoint, Landor says: "The field of History should not be merely well tilled, but well peopled. None is delightful to me, or interesting, in which I find not as many illustrious names as have a right to enter it. We might as well in a drama place the actors behind the scenes, and listen to the dialogue there, as in a history push valiant men back, and protrude ourselves with husky disputations." And again: "The business of philosophy," says Landor, " is to examine and estimate all those things which come within the cognizance of the understanding. Speculations on any that lie beyond, are only pleasant dreams leaving the mind to the lassitude of disappointment. They are easier than geometry and dialectics; they are easier than the efforts of a well-regulated imagination in the structure of a poem." And it is obviously Landor who says: "All religions in which there is no craft nor cruelty are pleasing to the immortal gods; because all acknowledge their power, invoke their presence, exhibit our dependence, and exhort our gratitude."

And finally, as perfectly mirroring the Greek spirit, and as containing the essence of that Epicurean philosophy which would pray all men to enjoy the present, its sensations and

12

ideas, and to count not upon the future, let us quote these graceful words of Cleone: "We have kept your birthday, Aspasia! On these occasions I am reluctant to write anything. Politeness, I think, and humanity, should always check the precipitancy of congratulation. Nobody is felicitated on losing. Even the loss of a bracelet or tiara is deemed no subject for merriment or alertness in our friends and followers. Surely then the marked and registered loss of an irreparable year, the loss of a limb of life, ought to excite far other sensations." The implications involved in these ideas are Hellenic to the core. Indulging our passions and emotions within rational bounds, and entertaining no vain regrets over the past and no foolish fears concerning the future, let us seek to extract from the fleeting moment all the honey, which, in the

way of lawful sensations and ideas
that moment can afford. Such an
ideal is æsthetic rather than moral.
It is the good, approached, if at all,
through the gateway of the beautiful. It is the being " made perfect
by the love of visible beauty "; and
its keynote is personal nobility rather
than devotion to one's fellows. Such
an ideal was Landor's; and never
has it been more alluringly conveyed
than in his most perfect production,
the *Pericles and Aspasia.*

IV.

LANDOR'S PLACE IN LITERATURE.

.

IV.

LANDOR'S PLACE IN LITERATURE.

AFTER the somewhat exhaustive treatment of Landor as a man of letters, the determination of his place in literature must, in our estimation, have already been made, at least impliedly. Toward the close of his life, in a letter to Lord Brougham, Landor himself said : " I claim no place in the world of letters ; I am and will be alone, as long as I live, and after." That he has, nevertheless, a place in the literary world is now undeniable, and that this place can be fixed only by a comparative estimate, is also true. Just as it is impossible, or at least unnatural, for a man to exist alone, a cheerless solitary; so is it likewise out of the question for an author to waive or forbid comparisons. Landor must therefore be tried by the same jury as his fellow-authors. And what is the verdict?

That there are limitations to his genius it were folly to deny. The most damaging one consists in his lack of spiritual insight. Wordsworth's intuitional poetry was always an enigma to Landor, who was wont to affirm, that, as the miner cannot delve far into the earth, so man cannot plunge into the abyss of speculative thought without directly reaching the void and formless, and cheating himself and others into the vain belief that nebulous rings, mere airy nothings, are habitable worlds. Landor might have been a student of Kant, considering the accuracy with which, in a literary

way, he conveys the impression that
supersensible realities, if perchance
they exist, are unknown. Landor
had nothing of that Oriental insight
which leads the mind to discover the
one in the many, and a God in all
the affairs of nature and man. " As
one diffusive air, passing through
the perforations of a flute, is distinguished as the notes of a scale, so
the nature of the Great Spirit is
single, though its forms be manifold,
arising from the consequences of
acts." Does such a conception possess meaning and truth? Landor
would have answered this question
in the negative.

Nevertheless, after making due
allowance for limitations, it must be
conceded that Landor has offered
some permanent contributions to
literature. His style alone must
insure the preservation of much of
his best work. Barring the fact of

occasional obscurity, arising from undue condensation and a lack of tact and of sympathy for the reader, and also barring the fact that his sentences are at times too regular for exuberant life and reality, Landor's style is flawless. It is characteristic and at the same time universal.

Passing to subject-matter, one can find no valid reason for supposing that Landor has not enduringly enriched literature by the choicest of his idyls, of his scenes in dramatic poetry, of his imaginary conversations, reflective and dramatic, and by his *Pericles and Aspasia.* Moreover, as the author of separate thoughts, which exhibit their extreme delicacy and beauty all the more clearly after they have been detached from their more or less prosaic surroundings, Landor has a special call upon our admiration. With the exception of

Coleridge, English literature is almost devoid of really fine *pensée*-writers—like Pascal and Joubert,—who, though they stand related to the philosopher as gardeners do to the geologist, and though they are more concerned about truths than truth in its unity and at the same time its ramifying multiplicity, yet are stimulating and suggestive, often eminently so. And it is in this capacity, as well as in that of idyllist, dramatic poet, writer of imaginary conversations and letters, that Landor must long maintain a notable place in the minds of those choice spirits who love beautiful conceptions and noble thoughts beautifully and nobly expressed.

APPENDIX.

As an attempt to give color to our rough sketch of the *Hellenics*, those poetic gems from which beam the joy, buoyance, and serenity of the world's youth ; the following idyl, which is animated, however inadequately, by a spirit and method of treatment similar to Landor's, is subjoined.

THE noon had passed, and Athens
    lay in light ;
The deepening, azure-tinted sky drew
    low
The vault of heaven ; the air was clear,
    so clear
That shadows of yon ivy leaves hung
    there,
Against the wall, more real than what
    they feigned ;
The steeper slopes made cavernous
    shades ; and all,—
Saving the olive trees, which looked
    afar
Like hoary clouds stirred by a gentle
    breeze,—
All was distinct, yet warm with drowsy
    life.

And drowsy was the murmur of the
  bees
In Myron's garden, and, within the hall,
Lygeia, Myron's daughter, spake in
  tones
That plashed the air in silvery ripples,
  spake
To Rhoicos, ever and anon tapping
His hand to emphasize her word. What
  was
She saying ? Who can tell what swal-
  lows chirp
In spring ! The lover's language is a
  tongue
Known but to one who loves ; its ca-
  dences
Are those of brook or breeze or ocean
  wave.

So there they sat, hand linked in
  hand, and smiled
And prattled at the simple bliss of it ;
Till Rhoicos, catching sight of shades
  that lay
Longer than four tall pillars whence
  they came,

Declared 't was time to seek the breezy
      porch,—
Lygeia having prayed of him to show
The path toward Thebes, and thence
      must he depart,
Before the shades were twice as long as
      now.

    As Rhoicos ceased, the shadows
      spread afar,
Their sun had sunk into a darkening
      west :
Since all the lamps in heaven must
      drearily burn
For nights untold, before Lygeia's eyes
Could glow again upon the eyes she
      loved :
Rhoicos must leave the flowers and pur-
      pling grape
Of vine-clad Attica, must leave the light
From sun-illumined locks and sky-lit
      eyes.
He must away, for duty urged him
      home
To a lone mother, watching, with tired
      gaze,

13

For him who now should be husband
    and son
Together : nor was it permitted him
To journey back to rugged Attica,
When wintry blasts were raging o'er the
    land,
For it was whispered in the agora
That Athens meant to humble haughty
    Thebes ;
And even then the Athenian archons
    looked,
With eyes askance, upon a Theban
    youth.
And Myron longed to keep his daugh-
    ter home,
One winter more, to gladden his old
    eyes ;
So he declared Lygeia was too young
To see the nuptial torch borne blazing
    forth,
And Rhoicos must await till vernal
    flowers
Strew bright the way from Athens forth
    to Thebes.
Hence were they sorrowful.

And as they stepped
Upon the porch, whose frieze and col-
    umns tall
Were graved by Myron's skilful hand ;
    Rhoicos,
That he might turn their speech in
    smoother ways,
Exclaimed,—one arm against a marble
    shaft,
The other stretched in front of him :
    " 'T is well
For thee to bide here where the far-off
    sea
Flows glimmering toward the shore, and
    as thou near'st
Yon sun-bathed cliff, to catch the
    glancing smile
Of waves, that dash the sea-weed, ochry-
    hued,
Into the hollowed rocks. 'T were sweet
    to tread
Such paths with thee as guide. Bright
    Thebes can boast
Naught fairer than yon glimpse of wave-
    bound wharves,

Where husbandmen have garnered dues
 of oil
And fragrant wine. Yea, harvest-laden
 fields
And softly swaying cypresses are
 touched
With mellow light, and all is passing
 fair.
The sky is swept of every cloud, save
 one,
That floats serene in yon vast azure
 deep.
A foolish cloud! the flaming chariot
 wheel
Of Helios will crush into thin air
The mist that goes unguarded and alone.
Lygeia, thou art such a virgin cloud!
And would an oracle might straight
 declare,
No gorgeous vapor, silver-lined, will
 rise
To seek this white-robed cloud, when
 I have gone
The dusky way from Athens forth to
 Thebes!

Lygeia, vow to me, no darkling cloud,
Though silver-tipped, 'twixt us shall
    ever lower."
(For Rhoicos thought of the Athenian
    youth,
With their smooth-rolling words and
    glances soft.)

To this fond talk of clouds, Lygeia
    had,
Like other maids, paid but a grudging
    heed ;
For she would draw his gaze down from
    the sky,
Nor would she have her lover find a sun
More lucent than her glowing eyes, a
    cloud
So sweetly shading as their down-turned
    lids :
So she cried, laughing : " Thou thyself
    art changed
Into a sombre cloud with a silver rim ! "

He turned, and saw that she had
    edged with chalk

The shadow of his form—with crum-
 bling chalk
That gleamed against the dull, time-
 weathered wall.
" Now, Rhoicos, what say'st thou of
 clouds with rims
Of silver ? Shall I not admire this shade,
That mimics thee, as torches do the sun ?
For, gazing at this shadow of thyself,
I can compare my stature with thine
 own,
Can see how passing tall and brave thou
 art—
Nor was thy shadow quite so tall as
 thou !
But look ! thine outline stands below
 the frieze
Whereon Athené Parthenos contends
For sunny Attica 'gainst dreaded lord
Of wind-lashed wastes, Poseidon ; o'er
 thine head
Athené, my protecting goddess, holds
An olive branch with spiky leaves, and
 smiles
Upon thee."

At these sallies Rhoicos laughed,
And said : " Thou should'st have made
    my shadow beam
Upon the goddess ; for 't was on her day
Of choric dance and festival, I first
Beheld thy face.

           I had gone by that age
When boys choose rather to play games
    with boys
Than tame their sport to girlish tastes ;
    and soon
My dreams gave vision of fair maids,
    their locks
Streaming or garlanded with hyacinth
And myrtle intertwined, who blithely
    tripped
With me to groves where checkered
    shadows play ;
When, one clear morn, while Eos yet
    upshot
Her burnished arrows 'gainst the fleet-
    ing gloom,
We rose in haste,—I vexed for broken
    dreams

Of tripping maids,—since we must reach
    that day
The pillared heights of the Acropolis ;
For on the morrow Athens held in
    pomp
Her choric dance and sacred festival
In reverence of Athené Parthenos.
'T was on that morrow I beheld you
    first.
Amongst the white-robed maids who
    celebrate
The glistering goddess of the wide-
    arched brow,
I saw one form that sent me to my
    dreams,—
I thought it was Athené in disguise :
And all the journey home that face
    would start
From every wayside bush, and gaze at
    me,
And set me longing for Athenian streets
And sweet processions of untroubled
    maids."
And thus the lovers talked, as lovers do,
Of nothing save themselves.

But swift the fields
Grew golden-hued. The reapers shade
    their eyes
And westward peer : they think of wife
    and child,
And gladsome leisure at the eventide.
Such thoughts were not for Rhoicos :
    he must leave
Lygeia ; and the laughter that outgushed
From rosy lips, he might not hear for
    days
Untold. Hence, plaintive were their
    parting words.

And as he wound his way above the
    slope,
He looked back long and wistfully ;
    and oft
His helmet shimmered in the glancing
    rays :
Blurred was Lygeia's sight, she turned,
    she cried
To Pallas, who upon the frieze upheld
Her olive branch above the outlined
    form

Of Rhoicos : "O thou virgin Deity,
May I not see my lover's form till suns
Unnumbered flaunt their streamers in
    the west ?
Is this fond outline of his vanished
    shade
The only semblance of his shape for me
To gaze upon, and gazing, dream of
    him ? "

   Myron, within the hall, was polishing
A statue of that goddess who arose
Refulgent from the silvery surge, and
    smiles
On lovers, Aphrodite, golden-haired ;
And when he heard Lygeia's prayer, he
    came,—
His beard by many winters frosted
    white,—
And smilingly he spake : "Child, I o'er-
    heard
Thy words to Rhoicos, when, in play,
    thou saidst,
That he was changed into a cloud with
    rim

Of silver, and, within two full-orbed
    moons,
Will turn this silver lining toward thine
    eyes."
At these strange words his daughter
    marvelled much.

    Far other words came to Lygeia's ear
Full soon—dread words that set her
    pondering,
Until her limbs grew tremulous with
    cold,
And stifling fear clutched at Lygeia's
    soul :
'T was rumored in the streets that Ath-
    ens meant
To war with Thebes, and ever and anon,
A citizen, with breathless speech and
    looks
Inquiring, hasted to the agora,
To learn the latest word.   Lygeia feared
For Rhoicos, yet she tried to choke her
    fear,
And tended Myron's wants, as was her
    way.

And then to rest her after daily
cares,
When night folded the land in slumber-
ous shade,
She would steal out to their cool west-
ern porch,
And watch Selené ride, fulgent or
veiled,
Through skies paven with ponderous
clouds, through skies
Whose paths were lightest air ; then
oft her dreams
Would turn to that glad day, when, hand
in hand,
Rhoicos and she might journey forth to
Thebes ;
And nuptial hymns resound and torches
flare ;
When, suddenly, a blighting fear would
chill
Lygeia's soul, and she would turn, and
scan,
With troubled eyes, the outlined form of
him
She longed for.

And oft Myron, musingly,
Would mark this self-same outline, then
        would go
Into his workshop, whence arose the din
Of splintering chisel and of rasping file.
In this slow, weary wise, the days
        dragged on.

.   .   .   .

The leaves have fallen on the Attic
        slopes ;
And after battle's heated rush, how soft
To wounded warrior is their kindly
        couch.
Right valiantly have ten score Theban
        youths
Withstood, from dawn to eventide, the
        darts
Dealt by Athenian hands ; but now the
        bloom
Of Theban chivalry is faded, gone.
The moonbeams fall on faces that a day
Before had smiled farewell to loving
        maids
And tearful mothers, faces that can smile

No more, but lie all bathed in cold
    moonlight,
Or sunk in Stygian shadow, when a
    cloud,
Scurrying athwart the sky, obscures the
    moon.
The wind is sobbing, sobbing, in the
    trees ;
And ever and anon, a faded leaf
Is blown upon a burnished shield, and
    dims
Its brightness.

        Glorious little Theban band !
Like heroes have ye fought against foul
    odds,
Nor was there one poor, craven soul
    that turned
His back upon the foe. By your proud
    names,
Will Theban fathers call their lithe-
    limbed sons ;
And mothers, taking on their laps their
    boys,
Will tell the story of your fortitude,

Nor will they fail to speak of him who
stood,
Staunch leader of the ranks, Rhoicos
the brave.

.   .   .   .

With lordly waving plume and brow
elate,
The Athenians enter now their city walls;
And all the streets are clamorous with
acclaim.
The elder warriors throw their armor off,
Glad to reach home once more ; the
younger men,
Each clad in greaves and breastplate,
hasten forth
To seek the timid smiles of those they
love.
And as the maidens catch their heroes'
tread,
Each heart beats quick, and blushes
come and go.

Alone, disconsolate, Lygeia lay
Upon her couch ; and endlessly one wail

Kept throbbing, throbbing through her
    soul,—no more
To see him whom she loved, no more,
    no more !
Not even might she hang his dented shield
Upon the wall, and scan its rusting face.

And as Lygeia lay there desolate,
Old Myron called her to the western
    porch,
Whereon the moonbeams fell resplen-
    dently,
And spake in mournful yet triumphant
    tone :
" Behold, my child, what I in jest had
    wrought ! "

There, motionless, she stood, fixed was
    her gaze
Upon a statue, silver-sheened and large,
Of purest Parian stone,—statue of him
She loved,—one arm against a marble
    shaft,
The other stretched in front of him, the
    head

Crowned with a wreath of glinting olive
    leaves,
Which, that same night, Myron had cut
    and twined.
'T was Rhoicos' self done to the finger-
    tips :
And yet Apollo, with his sun-bright
    locks
Rippling in air, shone not more glorious.

So did the goddess hear Lygeia's
    prayer :
Through weary, weary years her soul
    might hold
Long converse with his beauteous shape;
    and then,
When tears would flow, her eyes would
    catch a glimpse
Of that fair wreath of fading olive leaves ;
And pride and peace would fill Lygeia's
    soul.

                E. W. E., Jr.

www.ingramcontent.com/pod-product-compliance
Lightning Source LLC
Chambersburg PA
CBHW021226020726
47498CB00008B/2718